Vikings

The True and Surprising History Of The Vikings

(A Captivating Guide To The History Of The Vikings Age And Norse Mythology)

Anthony Lesley

Published By **Regina Loviusher**

Anthony Lesley

All Rights Reserved

Vikings: The True And Surprising History Of The Vikings (A Captivating Guide To The History Of The Vikings Age And Norse Mythology)

ISBN   978-1-77485-501-0

No part of this guidebook shall be reproduced in any form without permission in writing from the publisher except in the case of brief quotations embodied in critical articles or reviews.

Legal & Disclaimer

costs, and expenses, including any legal fees potentially resulting from the application of any of the information provided by this guide. This disclaimer applies to any damages or injury caused by the use and application, whether directly or indirectly, of any advice or information presented, whether for breach of contract, tort, negligence, personal injury, criminal intent, or under any other cause of action.

You agree to accept all risks of using the information presented inside this book. You need to consult a professional medical practitioner in order to ensure you are both able and healthy enough to participate in this program.

Table Of Contents

Introduction

Famous and Well-known Characters

Vikings are well-known by a variety of stories in modern society. There are stories that claim they are like comic book characters and others portray them as drunk, hairy thugs. A whole category of music is even created in honor of these characters even though we're all aware of the term as a whole and at the very least one image from popular culture however, few know anything about the people actually were and throughout history.

A misunderstood grouping of People:

There is no doubt that Vikings took on raids and were brutal plunderers, stealing communities along the coast to make money, but aside from those who managed to be crowned royal, the majority of them spent their time engaged in farming to support their family members. It might be more realistic to imagine them as people who were viewed as a scourge by their communities and were forced to take drastic measures to feed their family members. In some instances there was even a case of discrimination against religions that painted them in such negative light. If some of the stories and historical facts aren't true about them who were the Vikings really?

Advanced and intelligent Explorers:

Additionally, Vikings were highly skilled in combat techniques and general combat, however actually, they weren't the tough barbarians often depicted in stories or entertainment. Actually, their expertise technological advancements in making vessels and exploring the ocean provided them with the benefit of traveling across the oceans around the globe. Some were well-known and admired for their sharp wit and ability to think, which enabled them to stand out from the crowd.

The first people to discover large areas of our globe before anyone else, and included Greenland, North America, as well as parts of East Europe. While we might be enticed by the myths that we've heard about these people, they werein reality far more than that, as you'll discover in the next pages of this book.

The Vikings in this book are known for their often violent acts and plundering, however this isn't the whole story. They are also known for the way in which they shaped East Europe, North America as well as Britain. In the absence of Vikings at the time of their earliest days they could not be the way they are now. In actual fact we have the Vikings to be grateful for a large portion of the things we love in the modern age. Learn more about that, plus more within this guide.

Chapter 1: Erik The Red

Erik The Red is Erik the Red is a Viking that is most well-known within Icelandic and medieval mythologies for being the creator of the first permanent settlement in Greenland. Legend says that this remarkable Viking came into the world in 950 in the Southwestern region of Norway. Thorvald Asvaldson is his dad, and Osvald Asvaldson was the father. A family tradition of the Asvalds was born in the year Osvald was initially accused of murdering one of his relatives. Famous for his temperamental and sly personality, together with his hair and beard It didn't take long to earn his famous name.

The events that led to Erik being exiled from his home:

At just 10-years-old, father was exiled after he killed a person and then moved. Erik left his country in Norway in order to head to Iceland and so did his father. It was a great time for Erik's father as well as the family members for a while until Erik's staff members got caught up in a tragic accident which resulted in the home of his neighbor being destroyed. A neighbor's friend killed the servants in reaction to this. To regain them, Erik murdered some of his own men. The result was Erik being exiled from the region.

When Erik The Red was exiled from the country of Iceland in 980 Erik the Red made the decision to explore what was towards West (what is now referred to in the present times as the nation called Greenland). He set out for sea in 892 but had difficulty getting to the coast due to the amount of ice that was in the waters. To combat this the group travelled around the highest point of the country, and ended with settling in Iceland. Erik the Red chose to head back to Iceland after a couple of years and set up the first colony.

A dispute with a friend which led to chaos:

Then , there was problems for Erik. He decided to loan some beams adorned with Viking symbols and valuable properties of a mystical nature (according to pagan lore) to an individual named Thorgest who was a settler-friend of his. Then the day, when Erik tried to claim his property, Thorgest was unable to return the beams. Erik took them in and drove back to his home. In anticipation of a retaliation, Erik organized an ambush for the thief as well as his gang. The result was a huge confrontation that resulted in the deaths of two children of Thorgest. When the village court was held, Erik was banished again from the region.

Erik Sails to Greenland:

After this saga, Erik decided that he had had enough and decided to leave Iceland completely. He learned of a vast landmass to the west of Iceland that was discovered more than a century before by a seaman from Norway. This voyage had covered several miles of open ocean however the risk was mitigated by the modern designs of Viking sailing ships as well as the extraordinary navigation skills that were the work of Erik Red. Red himself.

Between 982-983, Erik was sailing around the bottom part of this huge and mysterious land mass and eventually landed somewhere which is now called Tunulliarfik today. Beginning at this point, Erik the Red used for the next few years traveling towards the west and north. He explored the regions and naming them in accordance with his own. He believed that the areas he visited would be perfect for breeding livestock , and he named the country Greenland to attract new settlers and visitors to the region.

The Continual Settlements become established on the Land:

After a few years Erik's sentence had been vacated and he made his return to the country of Iceland. It took less than a full year him to convince just a few hundred Icelanders that the new nation he was able to discover was an extremely promising place. In the next few months it was time to embarked on a voyage to the vast landmass, accompanied by more than 20 ships and about a hundred people. Some of these vessels were forced change course or were lost at sea, however 14 remained and the pilgrims set sail to form a few colonies.

They included the Eastern settlement as well as The Western settlement, as well as several smaller settlements were found between. Erik resided here with his spouse and four children. His sons were named Thorvald, Leif, and Thorstein while his daughter was called Freydis. The ancient sources say that the colonies survived the ravages of war and illnesses however, they never had more than 5,000 people. In the end, the colony were destroyed by the time of Columbus. According to sources, Erik died shortly after the beginning of the millennium. Probably due to injuries sustained from being thrown on his back.

Divergent Versions of Events in a variety of accounts about Erik's life:

There are a lot of similarities to the Greenlander series, including characters who return, as well as similar descriptions of expeditions, however, these stories do have distinctions that stand out. Erik the Red's story describes numerous expeditions in the Greenlander story as one long, continuous journey. A differentiator worth mentioning is the location they choose to decide to settle. In the Greenlander series the characters settle in a region known as Vinland The location will be discussed further in the tales of this book. In the story of Erik the Red two main settlements are created with one to stay in winter, and the other to relocate into during the spring, where they met with the

Natives in North America and encountered some difficulties and misfortunes.

Though different versions tell different versions of the events about Erik the Red's life, everyone are in agreement that he was an incredibly brave warrior and a great warrior who'll be immortalized in folklore for all time. There are a few different spellings for the same names throughout this book. This is due to the fact that the information is sourced from multiple sources, and spellings have changed over time due to the change in the perspective and history of storytellers.

Chapter 2: Freydis Eiriksdottir

While many, and even those who are fascinated by Vikings aren't aware of that there were Viking women. A recent study on burials of Vikings confirmed that there were of female Vikings than previously thought and that as much as 50% of Vikings may be female. The reason that this is considered to be the case is due to the fact that scientists are now analysing the remains of graves and not just the objects discovered in graves. There was a belief that the grave that had a sword inside belonged to the man who was buried there as well as that graves with a sword and a brooch inside were also a part of the male population and the brooch was an offering offered by an female. However, eventually it was discovered that graves containing the brooch and a sword most likely were the property of female Vikings.

Freydis Eiriksdottir was one them; she was her mother was Erik who was the Red and the younger sister of Leif Eriksson. Freydis was also a determined adventurer and traveler who ultimately made it to Vinland and won an enviable reputation for her bravery in

Vinland. Freydis is known, rather famously as pregnant Viking. According to some accounts, she was noble and brave and noble, while others describe her as cruel and uncaring. The next chapter we'll examine both versions and attempt to determine the cause of the differences in both tales.

The trade between Native Americans and the Vikings:

Leif Eiriksson, as well as his colleagues of Norsemen was on the shores in North America (which is currently called Canada) in the latter part of the 900s concluding an agreement with indigenous people who were already in the area. Freydis along with her husband went with Eiriksson to meet Native Americans of the area and they appeared eager to trade with foreigners. The Natives accepted visitors from the Viking tourists and offered animal skins to make fabric, as it was red, and the Natives were unaware of the process to create red fabric in the early days. This was however an uneasy relationship and peace was not to last for long.

An Unfortunate Mistake:

The colonists started to run low on the cloth red, they realized it was evident that Natives were keen on trading however they had nothing to trade with them, other than milk. This resulted in Natives experiencing a negative reaction to milk because they were not familiar with lactose, which led them to believe they were infected by Vikings. This caused conflict between the two cultures for a while. It got even more tense when the Viking bull was able to escape and started an errand before the Vikings were able to bring the bull under control. This scared all the Natives away. The Natives weren't seen for several weeks.

A Retaliatory Response to the Native Americans:

The Natives were able to row upstream making use of the river for travel and outnumber foreign settlements. They came up to waving and howling staves while the Vikings were able to stand in their stead. In the end, however they realized they were outnumbered and had little of a chance to defeat the Native Americans. They attempted to retreat and utilize geography to their advantage however, it didn't work as well.

The result was a massive gathering that forced Vikings to leave, but one of the Vikings did not want to participate. As they walked up to the native Americans Leif's child, Freydis, talked down about the capabilities that her fellow Icelanders from Iceland and requested that they hand her a weapon since she would likely be better at fighting than them.

Freydis's frenzied fear of Enemies:

The only time she received the weapon after she was already in the midst of her fellow Native Americans, after all of her friends had been taken away. After removing a sword from the body of one women, she struck her chest using the flat part of the weapon, yelling and pointing her chest at the enemy. It was then that the Native Americans quickly realized that their enemies were all dead but one was still alive and they were not eager to discover the reason she was acting. The sight of a woman who was pregnant striking herself and shouting at her enemies was an appealing scene, so they made the decision to leave and leave. This is the basic beginning to, middle and the end of the tale of Freydis Eiriksdottir as per one source.

The Greenlander Saga's account of Freydis Eiriksdottir:

Other historians offer another story. The above story comes directly from the Saga of Erik the Red and is among the only two reliable sources you can trust for information about Freydis's adventures and life generally. Another source, dubbed The Greenlander Saga, has quite an entirely different tale to relate. Although this source covers many of the similar instances in The Saga of Erik the Red, the Greenlander version portrays Freydis as a villainous, untrustworthy and manipulative. The stories portray Freydis as a woman who was had a marriage for wealth and by herself and never accompanied men on their journey to earn more.

In the story of the Greenland Saga, Freydis convinces two men (who are brothers) to join her on the journey to Vinland along with her, but she does it only to trick and then double cross them. Inventing a story of the brothers causing her to lose respect, Freydis tells her husband she must get revenge or she'll be leaving her. This results in her husband murdering the two brothers, as well as the brothers' male companions and Freydis finalizing the task by killing all the women in the group and the two brothers.

Following this, Freydis is said to have taken the vessel of the deceased brothers, and sifted their wealth, persuading everyone who was witness to these incidents to remain silent and then returned to the main group that was the Vikings. The fact is, this wasn't in the dark for long. Leif Freydis's brother could discern that something was wrong and obtained a confession of a few witnesses by beating them. When he uncovered the truth behind the incident, Leif decided not to take his sister's punishment, and the legend goes on to say that after the incident, nobody ever had anything negative to speak of Freydis.

The reason for differences Between the two Versions of the Story:

With the way this version differs from the original version, how do we supposed to find out what actually occurred? Historical researchers have spent some time exploring the specifics of the various stories and have discovered certain details that help clarify the matter. There is a consensus that the story of the second in the Greenlander Saga was, at least in part, the result of religious propaganda by Christians. The version depicts the pregnant Viking as an atheist who did not give in to Christianity and presents the story as an illustration of a terrible person who did not follow the rules of the church, similar to Jezebel, a Norse Jezebel.

This will help clarify certain details that don't seem to be fitting together, for example, Freydis thinking that just a couple of gifts would disarm those who witnessed her betrayal the public or Erik inflicting torture on people to obtain information while he could have requested it from witnesses. The version that was published has been modified to match the specific stories of the time.

The Legacy left Behind written by Freydis Eiriksdottir:

Even though it's not the most logical source an oddity, it is true that the Saga of Erik the Red is regarded by scholars of the past to be more reliable than other sources even though it's been proved to be an altered variant that was a revision of the Greenlander Saga. It is believed that the Saga of Erik the Red was an intentionally rewritten account of the events of the expedition of Vinland and drew heavily on The Greenlander Saga along with other sources, the majority of which are undiscovered or otherwise undiscovered in our time. Although the specific details of the tale that tells the story of Freydis are difficult to determine, if not impossible to establish They certainly echoed many stories of shield maidens. They were incorporated into the epics to be a deliberate attempt by historians who were studying Norse stories, perhaps to illustrate the things Norse women were capable of.

Chapter 3: Ivar The Boneless

Ivar The Boneless (or Ivar Ragnarsson), Ragnar Lodbrok's son was a warlord of his fellow Vikings and is said to have been extremely fierce and brutal. There are many opinions on the origins of Ivar's intriguing nickname, which we'll explore within this section.

It is believed that the Viking Based Origins of a Modern English Word:

The man that was ruler over an extensive area that is now encompassing modern areas of Sweden and Denmark is believed to be known as a "berserker". The term is used to describe Viking warriors believed to have fought in a trance-likestate of uncontrollable state of rage that later became the phrase "berserk" with its meaning contemporary English. The word "berserk" was derived from the practice of wearing an armor (known by the name "serkr" in ancient Norse) composed of the skin of bears ("ber" in the old Norse) in battle. in combat.

Characteristics of Ivar the Boneless

The old Viking stories tell that tell of Ivar being a man who had cartilage where there ought to be bone. He was handsome tall, tall, and smarter than his peers. The legend has it that his height made the men who surrounded him look like dwarfs. His arms are believed to be so strong that they could hold the most powerful bow, with more powerful arrows than the people whom he battled.

How did he come up with the Unique Nick Name?

It isn't possible to know the origins of Ivar's famous name from, because there's an array of opinions on the enigmatic "boneless" part of the epithet. Some believe that it was a rather cruel expression to describe his inability to love or the fact that he was not a person of desire or affection in his body, others have the opposite story. This name could be a reference towards the possibility that he was extremely flexible, given that an old poem describes Ivar as not having any bones at all. Certain Norse sources claim that Ivar was carried on shields by his soldiers which led some to believe that he was in a wheelchair. This is somewhat unlikely, but Ivar was a famous and well-known warrior. Other sources suggest they carried chiefs on shields in part of ceremony after victories.

"The Unfurling" of the Viking Raven Banner:

Together with his brothers Ubbe as well as Halfdan, Ivar decided to travel across the ocean to Britain and become the leader of the what Ango-Saxon sources refer to as"the Great Heathen Army in 865. The result was what will be known by the name of Invasion of East Anglia. Ivar broke and smashed the Raven banner that was used by the Vikings in the region. Legends tell us that it was crafted through the efforts of three Ragnar the Lodbrok's daughter. They are believed to have negotiated peace and offered horses to the invaders.

Invading and taking over York:

The year that followed, Ivar the Boneless led his troops north and captured York the city, named in the eyes of the Vikings Jorvik. At the time, Northumbria was under a state of civil war and King Aelle was crowned the throne from the previous leader, Osberht, who had rule for eighteen year period prior to the. In spite of the tension between the two men agreed to unite against their common foe and it took about four months. The springtime of year 867, they sped through the wall of the city and crossed into York. Then the Vikings came together and massacred all who ventured into York, capturing people who were on the walls that separated York. Two Kings, Osberht and Aelle were executed.

An Abyss of Snakes and the Brutal Blood Eagle Treatment:

Ragnar Lodbrok was dumped into the pit of snakes at the direction of Aelle. In revenge to the man who had killed Ivar's father Ivar, Aelle had to endure the most painful and painful death that she could imagine and that was the blood Eagle. It was the most brutal Viking execution and torture technique that folklore has described often. The blood eagle was executed by cutting the ribs the unlucky victim from their spine, tearing them apart so that they resemble wings, then by pulling out the victim's lung by putting them through the back. Then, salt is applied to the injured. The remnants from the court of Northern tribes was pushed to north. Ivar the boneless opted for Egbert to become Northumbrian's puppet king.

Ivar Smooth Talking His Way Out of Trouble:

The Great Heathen Army continued on towards Mercia in the winter, and arranged their winter residence in Nottingham. Burgred, the King of Mercia region, Burgred, asked for assistance from the King of Wessex (Ethelred) together with his brother, Alfred. Alfred then took a group of soldiers to take on Nottingham and head towards Mercia. But, the outnumbered Vikings were unable to take on the Vikings. The man referred to as Henry of Huntingdon recounted the events around 250 years after they took place and describing the specifics of the fateful incident in Nottingham.

Ivar noticed that the whole army of England was present and recognized that he was in the position of weakness. In response Ivar managed to speak easily and win peace with his English adversaries. He returned to York and stayed for throughout the year. Then the Mercians took the decision to pay the Vikings who had stated that they would return home to Northumbria in the autumn of 868. Then the Vikings were forced to spend winter in York. York. They returned in East Anglia, leading King Edmund to try to thwart the Vikings with force. The result was the arrest of King Edmund who was then brutally killed in Hoxne near Hoxne, a village.

A brutal execution to King Edmund:

The beliefs of the Vikings permitted and even encouraged the cruel treatment of those who believed in"the "White Christ" that they Vikings believed were cowards. King Edmund was steadfast in his beliefs and refused to defy the beliefs he held insisting that they were more important to him than the life itself. The King was then beat, in the midst of a cries to Jesus with clubs, and was then tied to the nearby tree. The Vikings were then able to kill him with archers until he died after which they removed his head. Edmund's body was not buried and the Vikings toss his head into the brambles that were growing around. This resulted in further plundering on a huge amount, the massacre of monks, and the re-election of monasteries.

Ivar's Pursuits in Dublin, Ireland:

When the year 869 came to an end, Ivar the Boneless set out to Dublin with the brothers Ubbe and Halfdan take over the reigns for the Heathen Army. Many believe Ivar was identified later as Imar Ivar, who was the creator and leader of the House Ivar that controlled the ocean close to Ireland and was the ruler of Northumbria. Together with Olaf the White who assisted in his lead the country at Dublin, Ivar began a massive attack on the country of Scotland. They were then reunited at a site known as Dumbarton Rock, which they conquered. The occupation lasted about four months before they eliminated the source of water, in order to eliminate of those living within the rock. Olaf The White as well as Ivar the Boneless decided to remain in the region during the winter and went back to Dublin with slaves as well as plenty of cash.

This resulted in the Vikings paying tribute to the King of Scots, Constantine I.

There are some reports that claim Ivar passed away in 873 from a terrible and sudden illness, which has led historians to believe the nickname he received may have stemmed from the symptoms of the disease. Some theories suggest that he could have suffered from an illness of bone brittleness from the beginning which is the reason for his well-known nickname.

The possibility of a discovery of Ivan's Remains:

A professor from Oxford University and his wife have suggested that an Viking warrior's nine-foot skeleton could be Ivar the Boneless's remains. The year was 873 and the famed Great Army was believed to visit Repton in the area where they stayed for the duration of the winter. In 1686 the huge Repton grave was first discovered through the efforts of Thomas Walker, a laborer. The grave was again covered and then forgotten for a long time. Ragnar Lodbrok's story states that Ivar was burial in the countryside of England.

It is not clear if the bodies of the Viking warlord belonged to Ivan who was Boneless is not the issue. The body that was dug up by the professor believed to be the body of a man who was between 35 and 45, appeared to be an significant person. In the area of the burial there were the remains of more than 200 bodies. The body was buried with the boar's tusk the hammer of Thor and an axe. An examination of the bones discovered revealed that the warrior was a victim of an incredibly brutal and violent death. His skull was adorned with two distinct sounds, likely caused by the spear. The nicks that he had along his spine suggest that he had been likely to have been disemboweled when he passed away.

Some Mysterious Questions Concerning the death of Ivar the Boneless:

Alongside these traces of a brutal murder The skeleton's marks reveal that he received an abrasive blow on at the top of his leg which may have removed his sexual organs. This could be why the boar's tusk was discovered between the legs of the skeleton, as a way of making the warrior's body complete. The earliest Viking belief held that dead bodies were not allowed into Valhalla until it was complete. Researchers have concluded that the body discovered was stabbed in the jaw, arm and thigh head and then disemboweled and that each of man's feet and toes were slit open. It is believed that the man could be murdered as a result of an act of revenge for being a victim of destruction to the church and monastery that was wrought in the name of Ivar The Boneless. This is, obviously, speculation and has been convincingly argued however it goes against the idea that Ivar had bones that were brittle. There are things that cannot be determined for certain regarding certain characteristics that characterize Ivar the Boneless, or even how the cause of his death, but we believe that Ivar was an incredibly ferocious soldier that deserves to be remembered throughout the decades.

Chapter 4: Egil Skallagrimsson

Egil Skallagrimsson, a farmer, warrior and poet of the Viking time. The Viking age began from 906 until 995 . He is the most famous character in the Saga of Egil. This epic saga traces the time period that spans from the mid-800s until 1000 C.D. The information below is based on a story of Iceland known as Egil's Saga. As with all sagas, many stories and variations exist.

The Possibility Disease that could be caused by Egil Skallagrimsson:

Egil was born in the nation of Iceland with Skalla-GrimrKveldulfsson. He was the child of a woman called Bera Yngvarsdottir. He was also the grandson of Kveld Ulfr. There was also an ancestor who was named Hallbjorn that was Sami who was from Norway. At the time Grimr arrived in Iceland and was able to settle at Borg which was the place where his father was put to rest. Egil created his first poem at only 3 years of age. The poet was famous for his wild and sometimes berserk behaviors that, when combined with his unattractive appearance and large head has led some to think that he may have been

27

suffering from Paget's Disease. It is a condition that causes the bones to get thicker and can result in blindness in extreme instances. There are also indications of this disease in the poetry of Egil.

Egil's Extreme Starts and Reactions as a Young Person:

At just 7 years old Egil was playing a match with a group of kids who resided nearby. He was furious when realized that he was betrayed by one of the boys. In response, Egil rushed home to take an axe and run back, smashing the head of the boy who had cheated. The moment came when Berg-Onundr refused to let Egil to receive his due share of the inheritance his father left to his wife. This caused Egil to fight Berg in a one-on one battle on an island nearby.

In the following days, Egil was insulted gravely and was killed by Baror of Atley in response Baror of Atley, who was an ally of Eirik Bloodaxe King and the ally of Gunnhildr, the queen. In response incident, Queen Gunnhildr ordained two of her sisters to kill Egil. In rage, she also ordered the killing of her brother, whom she previously had a good relationship with. However, Egil beat the royal brothers as they attempted to get closer to him.

The Exuberant Journeys and Pursuits of Egil in the Countries he visited:

In early spring, Egil prepared a huge warship and set off on the East route, where he accumulated many riches and was a winner in numerous battles. The peace he made lasted for a few weeks in Courland and also traded with men from the region. The identical year Harald Fairhair was passed conscious. With the intention of being able to secure his right to the throne and the title of King of Norway, Eirik Bloodaxe killed his own brothers. Then he declared the fact that Egil was wanted for being an outlaw in the nation of Norway.

The Murder of Egil's King's Son and the Queen's King:

Berg Egil's nemesis He gathered an army of men hoping to capture Egil and was murdered in the process. Prior to his escape from the country of Norway, Egil managed to murder Rognvaldr and Queen Gunnhildr as well as the son of King Eirik. Then, he pronounced an oath on the King and Queen, setting the head of the horse on a pole, and then proclaiming the curse. Then, he set the pole on top of a cliff, and remained it there, reversing around the head of his horse so that it faced the ground below. He then carved runes onto the pole. The queen responded by putting the spell over Egil and made him feel depressed and uneasy until they met again.

The Rival King and Queen of Saxon, England:

Following the exchange of curses the queen Gunnhildr and Eirik were forced to quit Northumbria as they were ordered to do so by prince Hakon to leave. Once they arrived in Saxon in England the two were set up as the King and Queen in opposition to the current King in England, Athelstan. At some point, Egil got shipwrecked in the region of Northumbria and discovered who was in charge of this country. Egil sought out a house belonging to a close friend known as Arinbjorn and the men were armed and prepared and marched to either the royal court, or Eirik. Arinbjorn advised Egil that he had to go and bow to the king and offer his head. He agreed then to present his case before the king.

The unsuccessful attempts of Egil to win over the King:

In the same way he was able to, Arinbjorn made his case to Egil and Egil composed a poem, and read it while he bows before the King. Unfortunately for Egil the King was not impressed with the performance. He informed Egil that his mistakes were far too numerous and extensive to be able to forgive that easily or even. Then, the queen Gunnhild demanded the queen to call for Egil to be killed. But Arinbjorn was capable of convincing the king not to go from executing him until next day. In accordance with Viking law it was not permitted to murder someone at night. Therefore, Arinbjorn advised Egil that he was to remain awake all night long to write a poem which extolled the opponent.

The next day, Egil appeared before the King and read out his masterpiece. He was stunned by how great his poem was that decided to let Egil to live even knowing that the man had killed the king's son. The complex and intricate structure of this poem provides an indication of what the it was like in that particular period of time. While there isn't much certain about the time and the people that lived inside it, poetic phrases remain.

The End of the Hard Headed Poet Viking:

Egil later returned to Iceland to stay on the farm with his family, and held power in the political arena of the region. He lived to be old, and died prior to the time that Christians became the rulers of his land. Prior to the time that the Viking died, he kept some silver in the house of an employee. Prior to the time Egil was gone the servant was killed by his servant, possibly in the hope of keeping the others at bay. A church for Christianity was built on the family homestead of Egil's and his body was later to be excavated and then placed in a different location. Legends say that the skull removed did not fracture when struck with an axe, leading scientists to think that the suspicions of Paget's disease were true of Egil.

The Legacy left Behind of Egil Skallagrimsson:

The man was a father to five children And later the clan of Myrar claimed that they were descendants of Egil. While Egil was an infamously tough and brutal soldier, Egil was also famous for his amazing poetic abilities and was considered to be one of the most famous poet at the time by a few historians. The poems written by Egil were the first Old Norse poems that utilized an end rhyme. It's unusual and rare for an Viking to be praised for his poetry and not his raiding abilities, however Egil wasn't the only person who enjoyed poems. Egil was a skilled writer when it came to writing beautiful poetry and also in the process of killing.

Chapter 5: Sweyn Forkbeard

Sweyn Forkbeard was born during the year 960. He later became monarch over England, Denmark, and parts of Norway and Norway. He was the father of Cnut the great and was the son of a man called Harald Bluetooth. Harald Bluetooth. Around the year 980, Sweyn rebelled against his father and took the seat on the throne. Harald was put into exile. He didn't make it through the for long, dying in the autumn of the year 987. At the time of 1000 Norway is ruled by Sweyn and, only a couple of years later Harald's efforts to become a king of England resulted in success.

The Early Family and Life from Sweyn Forkbeard:

Certain details about the Viking's history and activities aren't agreed upon. Certain scholars debate which details are authentic and what isn't, as there are a myriad of chronicles available. One source claims that the identity of his mother can't be determined and another sources her name with the clarity of a the day. Another source states that his wife's name is his and another claims to be an individual who is completely different.

There are many negative reports about Sweyn, one of which is based on texts by Adam who was from Bremen. Sweyn as well as the entire region of Scandinavia was said to have been observed by Adam with a sense of intolerance and lack of compassion. Forkbeard had been accuse of Adam of being the rebel as well as a pagan that detested and was a sworn enemy of Christians. He also asserted that Sweyn had betrayed his father and had removed bishops from German origin from Zealand in addition to Scania. According to the account from Adam, Sweyn was exiled by the German family members of his father. He was later was sacked by a king from Sweden known as Eric the Victorious who was the head of Denmark.

The personal offense of Sweyn's at the site of a massacre in England:

Students of the past have struggled to fully accept the assertions of Adam and his family, which includes the claim that Sweyn was taken into Scotland in order to remain there for 10 years. The historians could point out that to disprove this claim, Sweyn constructed buildings in Denmark at the time which included churches. Another story about

Sweyn Forkbeard's life Sweyn Forkbeard reveals that he participated in Viking raids against neighbouring England in the first 1000 years, to seek revenge on those who had killed Danish residents of England during a massacre that occurred in the year of St. Brice's Day. Forkbeard is believed to have been personally upset by these murders , and it is likely that his wife and spouse were among the dead Danish residents.

The Viking's Raid Participation Out of necessity?

Forkbeard attempted to lead campaigns across both East Anglia and Wessex in the beginning of the 1000s. However, the unexpected calamity of famine caused that he was forced to go to home in 1005. In the following years further raids were conducted and even the attack on England through the Vikings. According to historical accounts, it's not clear if Sweyn was involved in or backed these raids, however the king was not shy about making use of the disruptions caused by the army's actions. Some academics believe that the involvement of Forkbeard could have had a lot to do with the amount of poverty his situation was following the time he was forced to pay off a large ransom. The result was that he was desperate for the money he gathered from the raids. He could accumulate huge amounts of money this method. Then, in 1013 Sweyn has been said to be the one to have personally led the forces against an all-out English invasion.

The way The English Responded To Sweyn Forkbeard:

In the summer of the year, the king Sweyn was able to arrive with his troops in the region of Sandwich and quickly travelled to the Humber's mouth within East Anglia. He then travelled up to Gainsborough and met Northumbria as a whole , and Earl Uchtred who was bowed by the man. The inhabitants, in general who were part of that region of Lindsey Kingdom are all said to have paid a bowed bow in turn, followed by the residents of the Five Boroughs. Hostages were offered to him from all areas and he could tell that all of them had accepted his authority as a matter of law.

He believed that the troops must be equipped with horses and provisions which is why he travelled south with the largest part of the forces that were fighting. Then he crossed Watling St. and made his way to Oxford in the town, where the residents within the village also bow down to him and offered hostages to the man. Then they headed for the country of Winchester in the area where they received the exact same treatment and then towards the town of London probably expecting to experience similar reactions. However, the people of London didn't bow so easily, but instead protested.

The reason for this was that the Viking leader called Thorkell the Tall as well as King Arthur personally resisted his presence in the London city. London. This resulted in Forkbeard to head westwards towards Bath, the capital city. Bath and the city's citizens made a show of respect and offered them hostages. The citizens of London at this time were similarly obedient scared of what the retribution from Sweyn could be as if they stayed out. Then, Sweyn Forkbeard was named the King of England during the winter of 1013.

"Sweyn's" Short Rule and the Events that followed:

The kingdom of Sweyn was established and was based in Lincolnshire which was in the area known as Gainsborough. However, his rule did not last for long, and just one month after being appointed King, he died. The body was returned in Denmark to be laid to rest in a church was built by him himself. The location of the church was previously questioned as the tradition said it was in Roskilde However, more recent information made scholars believe that it was located in Lund in Scania (part of the present-day Sweden). The Sweyn's eldest son Forkbeard Harald II, took the throne, and became Denmark's King however England's fleet of Danes demanded something different. They wished for their younger brother, Cnut, to rule.

In England the council members rallied to demand returning a King that could remove Cnut from the region and this occurred in 1014, after Cnut's return after exile to France. The war only lasted for just a few years but Cnut returned to become the king in 1016. He also took over the throne from Norway, Denmark, Pomerania, Schleswig, and portions of modern-day Sweden. Cnut, the Cnut, the son of Sweyn, Cnut, and the children of Cnut, Harthacnut and Harold each ruled over English territories for more than 25 years. After Harthacnut passed away the throne in England was handed over to a different territory, which was the House of Wessex. It was in the form that of King Edward who was king until 1066.

They were the descendants of Sweyn and his daughter Estrid his daughter was the ruler throughout the years which followed and continue to reign today in Denmark. One of these relatives, a lady called Margaret of Denmark was married to a man named James III, joining together the bloodline of Sweyn to the royal family of Scotlandn in 1469. James VI, the Scottish man, then became the heir to the crown of England in 1603and heirs of Sweyn Forkbeard once more the rulers of English country.

A Synopsis of the deeds of the Sweyn Forkbeard Viking:

Whatever your view of Sweyn is the truth is that it's difficult not to be awed by some of his achievements. Sweyn was a rebel against his father in 987, becoming the king of

Denmark after which he shifted his attention to England in the year 987, where he racked up the coastline for nearly 10 years prior to returning back to his home country. Then , he began to attack his country of rivalry, Norway, at the new millennium. After he targeted Norway for a period of time and killed their king, Forkbeard took over and divided the country and repressed anyone from Norway who pledged an oath to the former king but was not Sweyn himself. In the same time when Sweyn's influence over Norway increased his influence, Sweyn's influence increased, the St. Brice massacre of Danish people living in England was committed. This was what prompted Sweyn to turn his attention on England and to avenge his country, his nationality and perhaps even his own sister.

Chapter 6: Erik Bloodaxe

Erik Bloodaxe is likely one of the most well-known characters in the story of Viking folklore, particularly on the Isles of Britain. Erik was the preferred son of the man called Harald Finehair. Viking epics praise Erik for bringing together Norway and then eventually to become the chief of the west region of the country after his father died. However, Hakon, his younger brother, was able to take the throne, and with his support of the people of Norway and was crowned. Erik was forced to relocate towards The British Isles. After Erik moved, he made use of his time to attack areas surrounding that region of the Irish Sea, including Scotland and later came to become the ruler of Northumbria which was known as the Viking kingdom. He passed away in 954 and along after his death was the end of Northumbria's independence. However, in the years following his sons were crowned King of Norway.

What is the origin of this Nick name come from? who was the Erik Bloodaxe?

Erik Bloodaxe has a famous name that is mentioned in contemporary sources, but he's left physical evidence of his legacy, such as coinage he created in his name within York. York. The character is also featured in later stories alongside her wife who's described sometimes as a villain. The name "Bloodaxe" is believed to have originated from his raids within what is currently in the United Kingdom, along with the infamous title of the last ruler of Northumbria to be independent. Similar to his close kin Thorfinn of Orkney The name Bloodaxe brings to mind the classic warrior Viking image of a giant and heroic, armed with an Axe.

A closer examination of the life of Erik Bloodaxe will reveal that his life was much more complex than the simplistic images created by stories. Bloodaxe had a renowned reputation as a fierce fighter, however, Bloodaxe was able to leave Norway to Hakon the brother of his, without a fight and was exiled out of Northumbria not just once however, but twice. Perhaps his name isn't as it appears. So, what is established about this guy?

What are the most probable assumptions regarding Erik Bloodaxe the Viking?

Certain excavations as well as further research have revealed the clearest image of what the modern-day York might be like at the time when Erik reigned over the area. The information we have about Erik's life in his homeland of Norway only comes from stories from the sagas. They can't be firmly believed for the period. However, while it's wise not to trust everything you read in the sagas of the present period, the details described are a general outline of events that do not reveal anything more than a little bit unbelievable about the person.

Together with these older epics, there's some Latin depictions of Norwegian Kings and their story. Much like the sagas of earlier times, they were written during the latter part of the 12th century which led to the notion of connection between the sagas of Iceland as well as the Latin historical records. The texts that are found in Latin are shorter and less magical than the sagas about the kings that were written in the beginning of 13th century period.

Erik was his father's most beloved and most likely the eldest child (of several) to Harald Finehair, the King. The stories of the saga assert that Harald was the father of up to 20 sons and was king over all of Norway. of Norway however, historians of the present have discovered that the kingdom was probably restricted to a specific part of Norway, instead of the entire nation as a whole. The king could be able to use his influence in the neighboring regions through alliances with rulers in the nearby region.

Erik Bloodaxe the Brother Killer:

The Kingdom of Harald although it was an adequate size, was not big enough to allow inheritance to the number of sons Erik was able to have, so Erik obtained his own inheritance in his own way, by killing each one of his siblings. This may be the reason that caused his well-known nickname. The tales in the epics describe his name as "Bloodaxe" However, a particular Latin source of information describes him as a killer of brothers. There is a belief that the term "blood" with this sense is referring to family relationships.

The reign Erik was able to exercise over the nation of Norway was unpopular and brutal, with his status as king being threatened by

Hakon who was the sole living cousin of Erik. Evidently, Hakon was brought up at an Athelstan court Athelstan which was located in England and later traveled to Norway via sea. Hakon set out on his voyage in the hope of claiming his inheritance rightfully, which led Erik to turn around and run away to England. According to the legend, Athelstan welcomed him because of the kinship that existed between Harald Finehair as well as Athelstan. Erik was later named the sub-king under the power of Athelstan and Athelstan of Northumbria. There is a possibility that Erik initially becoming the Northumbria's King on the advice of Athelstan seems to be contrary to Irish and English sources on the subject.

Different accounts of the life and legacy of Famous Viking:

According to the words of a few Irish Chronicles, along with an Chronicle of Anglo-Saxon depictions, Erik was crowned King in 948, a few years after Athelstan's death. Athelstan in the opposite from the will of Eadred Athelstan's younger brother. It is likely that the stories are muddled on specific particulars and facts that are relevant to this time. Erik is believed to have died under

Eadmund's reign. He was supposed to have reigned Between Eadred and Athelstan however, the story ignores his existence as Eadred entirely. Two names that are identical not being able to be distinguished doesn't mean that the other assertions in the story false. It is also worth noting that even though Erik isn't included in Anglo-Saxon portrayals of the reign of Athelstan There is no information on the person who was the person in charge of Northumbria for the benefit of Athelstan. This implies that it could be Erik in the end.

It is also possible to find evidence to support the narratives by the tales. A diary written by a person called William of Malmesbury discusses the relationship between Harald Finehair and Athelstan they are described as diplomatic, which doesn't disprove the saga's story. There are also the mention of Erik Bloodaxe in Caddro, an account of a Scottish saint's biography. According to the legends the saint was supposed on a trip to see Erik as well as his spouse in the present day city of York. The visit, which was believed to have taken place in the year 941 must occur prior to the initial appearing of Erik in the Chronicle published by the English-Saxons.

The Meaning of Erik's Dream on the Coins:

Erik's picture on coins could have a variety of meanings. The sword's design is a reference to an earlier style, which originated within the Viking kingdom of Northumbria. The decision of Erik to adopt this particular design could be due to an intent to show his status as the rightful head of the sovereign Kingdom of Northumbria. The epics of the kings show Erik being appointed chief by Athelstan to guard Northumbria against the Danish. The story of Egil tells us specifically that Erik's task was to protect against the Irish and Scottish the land.

This account of events remain in line with the reign of Athelstan and its overall outline as well as the information that is available. The power of Wessex expanding was a fresh threat to the kingdoms within the Isles of Britain and Athelstan faced an alliance that was repeatedly forged between rulers who joined forces. This included Scottish rulers as well as Viking King from the Dynasty of Dublin. Northumbria provided a required buffer zone between both the Scots as well as Athelstan. Athelstan and both sought allies to manage the area. In this regard, Erik becoming sub-king would seem to make sense. What we be certain of is Northumbria was under the control of different chiefs throughout this time period, as different forces were in charge of the kingdom.

The Kingdom is at war:

When Athelstan passed away in 939 Olaf Guthfrithsson seized the throne. Eadred as well as Edmund would be left fighting the Dublin Kings of the dynasty for the kingdom. The saga as well as the Anglo-Saxon version of events are in agreement with this tale, as well and the reality that once Athelstan passed away, Erik was making his own decisions, not being the Wessex sub-king of the dynasty. It's possible that the short period of time Erik had ruled were the result of fighting the kingship of Northumbria with his adversaries. The Anglo-Saxon chronicle provides evidence that Erik was recognized from the Northumbrian people as King. It's also evident that he wasn't able to use enough strength to secure his post when he was faced with resistance from Wessex as well as Dublin.

The Death and Demise of Erik Bloodaxe

At the age of 954, Erik suffered defeat and killed, bringing Northumbria's independence

Northumbria in the year 954 to an end. According to the Anglo-Saxon Version of the story states it was Erik was driven from the country by his adversaries, however the story in the saga claim that Northumbria was not rich enough to sustain Erik and his supporters, so he fled to go after his way across the Irish Sea and Scotland. Although this may have been partly due to the desire to pillage cities, the story is in line with Erik's alleged desire to share control with Dublin Kings of the dynasty, each of whom had an influence on the regions that bordered that Irish Sea.

The saga as well as the English versions both say that Erik was killed in battle. According to the saga version, the Earls from Orkney and several Kings from Hebrides. This is backed up through chronicles written by England that were later however it's difficult to locate specifics in contemporary source of data. A few sources later also claim that an ambush was responsible for the death of Erik which was commanded by Olaf's son Maccus. The name Maccus is not widely spoken of, though Maccus' name is mentioned in other sources that refer to the family of Dublin. It is possible that Maccus was King of Dublin's son, and also was a rival to Erik to be Northumbria's king in the 940s, which was the time frame.

Whatever the case, whoever Maccus is, it's likely that he must be doing what he did to support at least in part of Eadred who employed the strategy that was practiced of putting Viking rulers against one another. And, regardless of who the mysterious persona Maccus actually was, the demise of Erik brought an end to all rule by Vikings in the city of Northumbria. Many believe that this was the conclusion of the first age of Vikings however, the raids continued for several years. However, raids and settlements throughout Scotland, Ireland, and Wales continued to occur between the eras, which means that this time was not significant to the time of England.

Last words on Erik Bloodaxe are located in an older poem which mentions his entering Valhalla in a heroic manner and being greeted warmly by the gods in Valhalla following his death. It's likely to be a true account of an eyewitness this doesn't do much when it comes to our knowledge about Erik Bloodaxe's role as a persona of Viking time goes.

A Recap on the life and Times that Erik Bloodaxe was involved in:

Bloodaxe was Norway's heir. Once had enough of killing and robbing in his teens within the Baltic region, he headed back to Norway to try to take the throne to rule the region. The problem came from the fact that Erik had many brothers that shared the identical goal of claiming to inherit the crown from their father who died. In the end, Erik wiped them out using murder. But he didn't get the most crucial one that forced him out from the land. He built an impressive riches, encroached upon the Viking territory of Northumbria and enjoyed his reign as king, until the day he died in a gruelling battle in which his legacy was brought to an end.

Chapter 7: Ragnar Lodbrok

Ragnar Sigurdson Lothbrok was a well-known and mysterious Viking who is depicted in the sagas called The Tale of Ragnar's Sons and Ragnar's Tale. The story depicts him as an Viking ruler of Sweden as well as Denmark who is married early, then becomes widowed, and is again married, giving birth to at most two sons during the first marriage, and five more after the second wedding. Gesta Danorum is a documented account. is a book entitled Book IX that talks about yet another marriage. This could mean that Ragnar was not married to two but three wives in all and had two additional sons and daughters. The account also reveals Ragnar as having kids with women who were not part of his marriages.

The majority of the first half of these stories are set in Scandinavia and deal with relationships between Ragnar and his sons' deaths in the battle. The stories also discuss the possible revenge responsible for the deaths of these men. The stories that follow together with the work by Saxo discuss the adventures of Ragnar as well as his raids of

England as well as other areas of Europe. The story also relates Ragnar's death as well as the rétribution plot of his sons on the king of England that was believed to be the principal motive in the English invasion of the Great Heathen Army in 865.

The Legacy That Stretched Beyond Ragnar Hisself:

The children of Ragnar were given to through his wife went to grow into Vikings with their own famous names. Many of them were the kings of Scandinavia as well as having a significant influence on the politics of Europe throughout the remainder of the century, and to establishing multiple royal dynasties. The second part of the stories were set in Europe in the Christian period, which makes it difficult to link factual information with other writings about things that transpired during this time, specifically the chronicle from the Anglo-Saxon view. The chronicle's information seems to specifically refer to the sons of Ragnar as opposed to Ragnar and appears to be rather flimsy which makes it difficult to utilize them as evidence the fact that events from history are described in the sagas of these stories in a way that is factual. It is more likely that the tales in the sagas are actually based on real events.

The Meaning Possible Behind His Name:

The earliest sources of information from the past are not the usual sources for using both Ragnar and Lothbrok as a description of a individual. The first time they were mentioned with each other was found in a text that was written in 1120. This name has grown into an increasingly popular name in contemporary society, and even although Ragnar Lodbrok Sigurdson is the most popular name, Ragnar Lodbrok Sigurdson is given to his official biography There is evidence to support Lodbrok as well as Ragnar actually being husband and wife.

The famous Nick Name for Ragnar Lodbrok:

Anglo-Saxon accounts as well as stories describe the nickname Ragnar received, "Hairy breeches", due to his experiences in slaying a massive snake to save one his wives. The earliest versions of the tale do not include Lothbrok and Ragnar as a couple, and his sons are referred to as"the sons" of Lothbrok or the sons of Ragnar like they were two distinct people.

The Demise of Ragnar Lothbrok:

Later texts talked on later on the Great Heathen Army and their attacks motivated by revenge, which makes it appear like the incidents took place following Ragnar's death. Ragnar. However, more contemporary depictions of these events do not discuss the events as if they were related. This implies that Ragnar probably died before 865, probably in the 20 years before the year 865. The first source materials in English history, including the popular saga tales tell us that Ragnar was killed in his home in the Viking kingdom known as Northumbria in a cave full of snakes. The sources that followed later claim that he died by a snare in East Anglia, his murderer could be someone named Berne or perhaps a person named King Edmund. There are other sources that suggest it could be that he was killed in Denmark however, this isn't possible to say in a clear manner.

His death was somewhere between the two decades between 845 and 865, and at least two previous wives and almost 10 children, we can determine his death year. Some sources claim that he was born prior to 795.

This suggests that he must be no more than age 80 when the time he died.

Where was Ragnar Lodbrok's birthplace?

Denmark and Sweden is the two most probable places to have Ragnar's birth. Ragnar however, the regions weren't referred to by the same names in his lifetime. The King Ragnar, who became a famous character in the writings of historical writers as well as the sagas seems to be closer to Denmark than Sweden. Ragnar was regarded as to be a Viking one of Denmark can be believed that logically, it has Danish roots, but evidence of this is not available in the official record.

The marriages of Ragnar Lodbrok:

Aslaug Thora and Thora are the names the sagas use to women who were wives to Ragnar However, according to the Anglo-Saxon version of the events provides three wives names, including Lagertha having been the first one, then Thora and finally Aslaug as the final wife. According to the Anglo-Saxon version of the events declares that Ragnar had an unborn child who was out of the wedlock and this child's name was Ubbe.

"The Daughters of Ragnar Lodbrok:

An eleventh, or the 12th centuries states the 11th or 12th century says that Ivar Ubba and Ubba were the sons of the man together with three sisters that were not named as well as the Saxo depiction claims that Ragnar had two daughters and one son with Lagertha who was his first wife as per this information source. The characters profiled with no name who are believed to be the daughters of Ragnar are grouped to form a group of unknown daughters of the Viking.

"The Sons of Ragnar:

Ragnar's Tale mentions Rognvaldr along with Hvitserkr as children of Ragnar However, modern sources do not mention them in this manner. Some believe this could be due to Rognvaldr was likely the son of Ivar. The Anglo-Saxon version refers to Erik, Hwitserk and Ragnald as the sons of Ragnar Their mother was one named Swanloga. It is possible that Swanloga is merely a name for the wife of Ragnar who was referred to as Aslaug from other writings. It's impossible to say to be certain if they are the same person or not.

The Legacy left behind by Ragnar:

The epic story of Ragnar's Tale includes, in addition the names of two other sons Ragnar shared with Thora his wife of the past. Contemporary sources don't mention these sons in any way, but it could be because the stories of their parents are available only in Scandinavia and not elsewhere. Alongside these sons, sources which were later added also link Vikings with Ragnar by referring to Ragnar's direct children or listing them as siblings of the sons listed. They've also been put together into a single grouping referred to as unconfirmed sons of Lothbrok. No matter what is established we can be certain this: Ragnar Lothbrok, or whoever this mysterious figure was made a significant influence in the Viking world via his bloodline as well as the events that occurred during his life. The figure will be remembered for the rest of history, not only in Scandinavia and beyond, but also in the all of the world, as his name continues to be a fixture in contemporary, popular culture.

Chapter 8: Gunnar Hamundarson

Gunnar Hamundarson was a chieftain in Iceland during the 10th century. He was is the son of Hamundr as well as Rannveig. He had three brothers and sisters; two brothers and a sister. He was also married to a woman called Hallgeror Hoskuldsdottir. Gunnar was third spouse of Hallgeror. It was reported that she killed both previous ones, however the reality was that she was the one who killed her first husband. Gunnar's acquaintances considered her marriage unwise because the marriage was not founded on an ethical basis but rather lust.

Famous Qualities from Gunnar his Viking:

The Viking is known for his incredible abilities in combat, and his near-invincibility in combat. According to the legend, Gunnar was athletic and strong and could jump in the air to the top of his body while wearing armor. He was an archer of the highest quality and throwing stones, having the ability to strike enemies directly in the eye at great distances. He was also a master in the pool and couldn't be beaten in any sport by any other player. Gunnar was adamant however he was always friendly and offered great advice to his colleagues, using an easy and gentle speaking voice. Many thought he was unintelligent due to his soft style of speech but his profound knowledge and shrewd insights tell a different story and show that he was smart and proficient in combat.

Gunnar was a faithful friend who enjoyed good company. Gunnar was always called very attractive by the people who lived around him. Gunnar knew a good ally known as Njall whom he made frequent visits to for guidance. A few days ago, Njall offered him advice to hold back from killing two other men who were from the same bloodline that would result in Gunnar's tragic death. Amazingly, the prediction proved right. Gunnar killed two members of the family called Gissur the White. This prompted the remaining family members to take revenge on Gunnar. Njall once more advised Gunnar the advice of saying he needed to go to a different country in order to avoid the family that was enraged. In the beginning, Gunnar had the intention to leave, but he was said to have seen the home he had inherited in the distant away distance before he left. He was so fascinated by his home and its splendor that he decided it was his home although it's not clear if this was an intentional decision made by Gunnar to sacrifice his home. Whatever his motives the fateful choice resulted in his death which was followed by an epic fight.

At first, Gunnar was able to defend himself from attackers by using his amazing archery skills however, the bowstring he was using broke as he was fighting close. In this moment the couple pleaded with their wives to loan him hair from her so that to repair his bow but she declined in retribution, considering that the previous time he had slapped her in retribution for taking. That meant he was forced to stand up to his adversaries one-on-one in close combat. He was killed shortly after.

Gunnar Hamundarson, a character from folklore, is often described as the hero who is illumination in the sagas of Iceland which is in stark contrast to some of the more dark heroes, such as Egil Skallagrimsson for instance. The strength, courage and heroism that characterize Gunnar are, naturally exaggerated as any fiction is but he does not have any flaws that are immediately apparent or evident within these tales. In all the heroes in the Icelandic epics, Gunnar is likely among the most revered by his zeal, courage in the face of evil, virtue, and devotion to his country and the beautiful scenery. However, for certain modern-day Icelandic residents, Gunnar is considered a cliché character that is used to describe difficult to believe traits or over exaggerated characteristics of people.

Gunnar Hamundarson and his Life in summary:

Gunnar was a legendary hero from the sagas of the North and, based on his impressive skills with the bow and sword it is believed that his skill in fighting was the reason his name was made in famous tales. Gunnar is known as equally deadly with his sword using both hands, which gives Gunnar a distinct advantage over the other fighters. Gunnar also claimed to have never missed his target when he was aiming at anyone. Gunnar attacked the coasts of North and consequently, had a similar fate to numerous others Norse individuals and Vikings.

Chapter 9: Bjorn Ironside

Bjorn Ironside was renowned as one of Sweden's kings that lived during the ninth century. He was believed to have been among the first rulers and the founders of a dynasty that existed in Sweden known as"the Munso Dynasty. Bjorn was the child of the princesses Aslaug along with Ragnar Lothbrok. He was the second-eldest child in the family, following Ivar The Boneless. Bjorn's three brothers included Ivar The Boneless Sigurd The Snake-in-the Eye, as well as Hvitserk. There were also three half-siblings named Fridleif, Erik, and Agnar.

The successful Raids of the fearless Bjorn Ironside:

A fearless and fierce warrior ruler, much as Bjorn Ironside's father, Bjorn Ironside pillaged and took over many areas, such as England, Italy, Spain, France, and even portions from North Africa and Sicily. His life's historical accounts mention that Bjorn as well as an ally known as Hastein (who has been believed to be an alleged mentor for Bjorn as well as one of Ragnar's children) took over the land that was French and then headed towards to the

Mediterranean coast. After having racked the beaches of the nation of Spain The men then headed home to France to pillage more and then headed to Italy for a visit to Pisa.

They realized that they couldn't go in the same way after they entered the gate of Luna which they initially believed as Rome. After that, Luna as a city Luna was to be one of the most important accomplishments that was accomplished by Bjorn Ironside. He had snatched the entire city with his wits, which is one of his most famous traits which is the primary reason for how famous his name is now.

A sneaky and tactical entrance in Luna's City Luna: Luna:

The first time, navigating the wall of Luna was not an easy task for Bjorn and he needed to find a new way to gain entry into the city. The result was that he sent his men to inform the city's bishop that he'd passed away , but that he had made the decision to change his faith of Christianity prior to his death and was wishing to be given an interment on the consecrated ground. In response the city allowed the body of the deceased be taken to it by a tiny group of men (who according to some accounts, had swords hidden beneath their clothes).

When the body was brought into the chapel, Bjorn jumped out of his burial container, shocking everyone around him as he ran through the city's gates. He then opened the gates to let his army to enter and took control of Luna. Luna. The strategy employed by Bjorn is believed to be the work of his mentor who was possibly his, Hastein. After he had assumed control of his city Luna, Bjorn and his group of Vikings attacked the coastal regions in North Africa, along with Sicily.

The Attack on Bjorn's Fleet of Ships:

Everything seemed to be good with Bjorn and his men and they had had many successes with their raids. As they set off on their way back to their home they encountered naval commanding forces in their home in the Straits of Gibraltar, which could alter the direction of history for a few of the soldiers. It was not a happy occasion in the life of Bjorn and his army as they were attacked by a weapon called Greek fire which is a weapon that remains burning on any surface, even water. The ruthless weapon destroyed more than 40 ships belonging to Bjorn's Viking fleet.

The Love of Ragnar Lothbrok

Bjorn Ironside as well as Ivar the Boneless achieved massive and impressive success in their raids throughout the Mediterranean and across Europe. This caused Ragnar Lothbrok, who was angry with his sons and he decided they should not be ruled by the kingdom of Sweden. Instead, he appointed a person to become a surrogate king, named Eysteinn Beli and sailed into the open seas to take over the Northumbria kingdom, hoping to besiege King Aella who was a long-time adversary of his. Ragnar was unfortunate for him in not paying enough to the quests and was perhaps swept up in distracted by his feelings of jealousy over his son's accomplishments. This is why Ragnar did not attack Northumbria without much planning and only with only a handful of soldiers.

A Different Version of the Story:

In a different version of the same story, Ragnar chose to attempt to overthrow the throne of King Aella not due to his jealousy over Bjorn and Ivar however, he was angry with and disdainful of his wife, and was also displeased with his song Hvitserk and Bjorn as they had revenged Agnar and Erik who were their brothers without needing Ragnar to help. Agnar Erik and Erik had wanted Ehsteinn to follow their orders because they were brothers of Ragnar and Eysteinn Beli informed them that he was going to consult with chieftains from Sweden for an answer.

The Swedish chieftains, however, apparently did not agree with this request , but then instructed them to be sacked. Because from this incident, Erik was caught to be executed later (by his own choice because he was so depressed about losing) as well Agnar was executed at the same time. Ragnar was overcome by his pride, and was eventually caught and killed by Aella. Some versions of the story claim the man died of an illness (possibly dysentery) Some accounts mention that the king tossed the man into a pit.

His journey to become King and the Revenge of Ragnar:

When Eysteinn Beli fell Bjorn was officially crowned Sweden's king. He as well as his siblings were able to launch an assault on

Northumbria in an effort to get revenge on their father. Unfortunately , for them, the plans didn't work, because the forces that were ruled by King Aella were much stronger than the ones from the Vikings. The oldest of the brothers, Ivar, known to be the most shrewd of all the rulers in the time of the Vikings He let his brothers be aware that he was already aware that the fate of their father would be this way, and that he was going the King Aella to request the chance to reconcile.

As a response, Aella gave Ivar some the land to build York on. The next few years, Ivar the Boneless gained an increasing position among the Englishmen. Once he had decided it was the best moment, Ivar told his fellow brothers that it was the right time to take on Northumbria once more. Together with other men Ivar had united to accomplish the mission and gathered together for the task, the Vikings attacked the region and were able take the King's life. The brothers took a while to discuss which method of execution was the best for the King. They eventually chose the blood eagle method, which we have discussed in this book. They sat in the midst of watching as the king passed away.

The Repercussions of the Death of their father:

When their father passed in death The children of Ragnar divided the kingdom into two and led Bjorn Ironside to be the head in the two kingdoms of Sweden in addition to Uppsala. Bjorn was eventually crowned with two sons, Erik as well as Refil. Erik was to become the next king of Sweden following the death of his father. Bjorn is the person who established the House of Munso in the nation of Sweden that we refer to as"the Old Dynasty and which ruled across the country for a lengthy period of.

Generations of people lived this way until they eventually were required to quit Sweden after a period of war lasted for an extended period of time, and continued until the end in the 10th century. In the end, the Munso Dynasty would eventually be the supreme house of Denmark. The name for this area was derived from an island that is that is believed to be the burial site of Bjorn Ironside.

Chapter 10: Harald Hardrada

In the period between the eleventh century Vikings were in the end of their time of plundering and fighting. When they were defeated and humiliated by King Alfred in the 11th century, their defeat by King Alfred, Vikings (more specifically, the Danes) were capable of advancing and taking control of a large portion of the land of England in accordance with the orders of Cnut who was a Danish ruler. In reality, these actions led to the creation, for a short time period an empire in Scandinavia that was a fusion of Denmark, Norway, and England around 1027 A.D.

The Separation of European Countries and What Resulted:

But, all of these nations soon broke into two and each gained its individual independence (Ireland was free at the time, but it was not yet). In England it was asserted as the dominant country by the Anglo-Saxons shortly after 1040 A.D. This was largely consequence of an pattern which saw Vikings who were able to raid in different ways, and then being often defeated by frontier soldiers across both France in France and England. Furthermore the pagan-influenced fervor of these people was diminished and dulled by Christian values within the central regions in Norway in Norway and Denmark.

At the time of 1015 A.D., Harald Hardrada was born in Norway. The place was known as Rinerike which was in the peak of the Viking Age of time. Harald was the son of an individual named Sigurd Syr, a successful chieftain, who was from the fertile and agricultural areas located in the north Uplands in Norway. Harald's family believed that they were closely related to a person named Harald Fairhair, the very first King of Norway according to legends and legends.

What the Claims of Relation could have meant:

The claims could have been made after Harald Hardrada actually was alive in order to justify or justify his actions in his early days of existence. However however, it is important to know that Olaf Harald's half-brother was appointed Norway's sole king in the year 1015. He had his support of five chieftains. On the other hand Harald's family Harald was at war over Norway's crown. Norway which King Knut of Denmark Danish King Knut took from 1029 A.D.

There was discord between supporter of King Olaf as well as Harald's family Harald which eventually resulted in Olaf's exile. It wasn't long before Olaf returned in 1030 A.D., and started creating plans to claim the crown crown of Norway. Harald was steadfast in his support for the claims of his half-brother and was able to bring together hundreds of soldiers from the adjacent Upland region. The brothers later fought at an engagement during the heat of 1030, but didn't prevail unfortunately. Olaf died and Harald, who was then a teenager, Harald got hurt quite severely.

Harald's Brave Adventure Across the Swedish Mountains:

Injured and shaken by the incident that had occurred Harald, who was 16 years old, was shaken and injured. Harald was unable to find the right place to retreat to and get back the safety of. While his odds were not looking good, he did locate a quiet farm located in the East of Norway to seek refuge. A couple of weeks passed, and it was possible for him to heal well and move north and traverse over the mountainous regions of Sweden.

Harald Hardraga Making his way to Kievan Rus:

In the end, after one year was passed since the war which claimed his half-brother's life and caused him such a serious injury, Harald Hardraga found his way to Kievan Rus. The region consisted of a collection of towns and trading villages of Slavic nature that spread across Ukraine in addition to Russia. In the past, the settlements there were controlled by the Rurik dynasty. Rurik which were Swedish initially, but they had been able to mix with the population in the years since. It was a blessing for him that the grand prince of Rus, Yaroslav, openly accepted the Norsemen as it was clear that Harald was half-brother to Olaf. Olaf was a refugee at Kievan Rus during a time after his exile.

Harald as the Captain of Military:

Furthermore, Yaroslav employed Harald as one of the commanders of his army in view of the condition of the army in the region at the period. In the midst of the new rank and responsibility, Hardraga proceeded to make an impression on the world. He faced off against adversaries like the nomadic tribe known as the Pechenegs as well as The Chudes of Estonia as well as the Poles. There are also stories of Harald's attempts to court Yaroslav. Harald tried to marry the daughter of Yaroslav but he did not get much luck.

Harald is a young Harald taking a brave and risky chance:

In the end, however the prospect of growth to the top of Kievan Rus became a source of boredom for the young Harald Hardraga, and he began to feel uneasy. As his 20th birthday just come and gone He decided to try his hand at. He gathered an army of 500 supporters, and then led the group up to Constantinople known as Miklagard in the eyes of Vikings. The risk was having a positive result and working very well for Harald and he ended in being hired as an elite guard for the Roman Emperor in the region.

Unsurprisingly, the "Viking" was steadily promoted in the ranks through campaigns. The campaigns brought his young "Viking" towards Iraq as well as Asia Minor, where he had a great time in activities. He also travelled to Jerusalem in the belief that he was the one to oversee an agreement for peace with and the Byzantine empire and Fatimid Caliphate. In 1038 A.D., Harald was officially designated as a nominal head of the Roman army that was commissioned to conquer Sicily that was, at the time, was under the supervision of Muslims. At the time, Harald was an experienced guard, and could fight alongside prestigious mercenaries such as William Iron Arm, the famous historical character.

This is what we call the Climate of Nations and Politics today:

The strategies and military expertise of these soldiers allowed them to gain control over more than four kilometres in Sicily from the grip of Muslims. However, their success did not last long, as there was an rising uprising which was beginning to take place in the south of Italy. In the south, Eastern troops of Rome were swiftly defeated by rebels in the battles which ensued. The result was Sicily being taken away from the control of the Roman populace. In 1041 A.D., the guards of Varangian were relegated to the territory of Constantinople. The same time, Hardrada was engaged in an important mission to bring an rebellion in Bulgaria to rest. However, by the end of the year, the political machinations that governed the Byzantine empire had caught up with Harald especially in relation to the demise of Michael IV, a patron Emperor.

Harald In Legal Trouble Again:

In the subsequent battle between Zoe who was an empress at the time and Michael V, a new Emperor, Harald was locked up for violating the law. The exact reasons what caused this incident aren't clear as different sources have claimed different motives. The reasons vary from killing the emperor, or offending him, to an individual for defaming them. However Harald was not too long away from being released. Harald was able escape and be released from jail after which he joined in a quick and decisive battle with the emperor's guards with rebels. Harald was extremely fortunate, as he had the success of his efforts. The new Emperor, Michael V was taken down and blinded by Harald and let the rebellious parties go free.

Harald's Escape From the Roman Empire of the East:

While victory was sweet to Harald however, it wasn't long before him to have poor luck with regard to the royals again and this time, he was with Zoe, the queen. Zoe was the empress of Constantine IX, a co-emperor at the time. In recognizing the uncertain state of the political landscape of the Byzantine region in the period, Harald the Viking made the decision to head back to Norway where he was born leaving Constantinople in the dust. When the princess Zoe refused to allow him to go, and was wishing for him to remain at his job as guardsman, Hardrada made the choice to take advantage of the Black Sea as an escape way from to the Roman Empire in the East.

Harald together with a group of men who accompanied him, picked two vessels to make their risky escape. Unfortunately for them one of the ships was sunk right next to the famous monument depicting Constantinople's cross-strait chains. But, Harald knew how to escape from difficult situations and with some luck and wit, it was able to stay clear of being caught by Romans by directing his excellent ship in 1042 A.D. to get him back to the region in Kievan Rus.

The Amazingly Large Richess from the Viking Harald Hardrada:

While the tales that tell of Vikings in sagas generally differ, and offer different descriptions of the warriors of in the past, certain details have a common thread. The riches and spoils amassed through this specific Viking during his time at his time in the Byzantine court are just a few of the particulars. He also had a lot of prosperity by accumulating wealth through battles of the day. According to some reports, Manglabites was even his prize the top position for guards that was higher than his previous job.

His Final Success, He was married to the Grand Prince's daughter, Elisiv:

The majority of Harald's significant finances and records given into Yaroslav, the prince of the throne who was secured for safety reasons. Then, when he returned to Rus to renew his efforts to win over the love of Elisiv Yaroslav's daughter his efforts proved successful. Even though the Viking wasn't an official princess, Yaroslav was likely impressed by his wealth and eventually made the decision to let his Norseman to get married to his niece.

In 1046 A.D., Harald Hardrada is now more skilled in life and battle, took the decision to return to his homeland , using important cities for journey. This include Novgorod as well as Staraya Ladoga. From the port of the second place, Harald acquired a ship filled with gold and treasure and was able to reach Sigtuna, Sweden, using the sea.

Unexpected differences back in Scandinavia:

Unfortunately it was the political climate not what he expected for Demark and Norway in particular, and was undergoing a major change in the years when Harald was engaged in military operations all over the world. This means that the King Cnuts sons had both died and the throne in Norway was handed down through to the lineage of Olaf and yet again. The throne was now the property of Olaf's son-in-law called Magnus The Good. The majority of the time, Magnus the good was believed to be a competent king who had overthrown Sweyn Estridsson, who was who was regarded as a pretender within the realm of royal power.

This led to the belief which Harald Hardrada had to be in a position that was unusually grave, in part because the throne in Norway ought to be believed to have was Harald's and was taken over by an outsider. However, this didn't stop him from making an attempt, and the spirited Norseman took the initiative to take on the status quo and swiftly making an alliance together with Anund Jacob, the king of Sweden and a third person called Sweyn Estridsson. The two forces formed a coalition and began to make attacks along the coastline of Denmark in an attempt to intimidate their enemies while simultaneously it was proving they were Magnus the Good was unable to come up with effective methods of fighting back and protecting the inhabitants of the region. Invincible by the attacks of the water, King's advisors decided to compromise on a political level. This gave Harald the power to be the ruler of Norway and Magnus The Good was to become the leader of Denmark as well as the ruler of both regions. The second part of this was designed to ensure that Magnus in a position higher than Hardrada.

Sweyn Estridsson, and Harald Hardrada Butting Heads:

The consequence of this was both men established their courts independently and never got together to discuss about the state of their respective states. However, by the year 1047 A.D., Magnus had died and wasn't in a position to create a rightful successor of the crown. In view of his dislike of the intrusions and misdeeds that were the fault of Harald, Magnus had thought ahead and designated the legitimate successor to the Danish throne prior to his death. The successor was Sweyn Estridsson, who was a former close friend and ally of Hardrada. The decision eventually caused Sweyn Harald and Harald to battle over the area which was Norway as well as Denmark. This resulted in a lengthy battle against Sweyn and Harald. However, the two in 1064 A.D., signed an agreement to end the war.

The Hardrada's Hand in the Seizing of York:

In the event that a man by the name of Edward the Confessor died in 1066 Hardrada claimed that the bloodline of his was entitled for the crown of England because it was promised to them by the King of Hardicanute. The king was head of England for two years beginning in 1040 A.D. In 1066 A.D., Harold of

Wessex's younger brother went for a meeting with Hardrada at the border of Norway. The two men sat down and discussed their plans. the decision to enter England in the early autumn. They also brought together a few hundred ships to cruise the close coasts and plunder the areas around. One of the plundering activities was the action of setting Scarborough to blaze. Then, around mid-September the soldiers were capable of taking off the armies of Morcar. In just a few weeks later, the men took over York.

The death of Harald Hardrada the Viking:

In the latter part of September, a large force of soldiers came to Yorkshire and astonished the two Harald Hardrada and Tostig. Because it was so hot out it was warm outside, the Norsemen were wearing their mail-stamp and shirts. The soldiers of England were capable of taking these men to the ground easily, killing Tostig as well as Hardrada. Norway suffered a lot of losses the day before, and of the few hundred ships, barely more than 20 made it to the journey back to Norway.

Chapter 11: The Historical Resources

The language spoken by those who were Vikings used to be Old Norse, which during the Viking Age was written as runes. The information we have about them is derived from sources like documents from the medieval period, archeological discoveries as well as surviving folklore. Many of them have been lost and what is known to us in the course of time has been made possible by the laborious efforts of many historians who have gathered and compiled the diverse items from Viking, Norse and North Germanic history.

The literary works from the Old Norse language, from the ninth to the 15th century AD is the most significant contributions to the understanding of Viking the history of the Vikings. The people of Iceland and Scandinavia adhered to their religion of choice more than the majority of Germanic people. They were also better in the preservation of their stories or customs when Christianity was declared to be the only official religion (as it was in Iceland around AD

1000). The modern historians believe that those Old Norse poems, sagas and treatises as the most important narrator in Scandinavian history.

Norway as well as Iceland were also major locations for the development of literary works relating to Viking mythology. In Iceland there was a flourishing poetic tradition created two significant treasures that illuminate the myths as well as their historical context The Poetic Edda and the Prose Edda. It was written mostly in the thirteenth century by Snorri Saintluson (an Icelandic scholar and politician) and a number of anonymous authors, these manuscripts bring together the long-standing oral history of kennings and skaldic poetry.

The Poetic Edda

The name "Edda" is ascribed to Snorri Sturluson's poetry, the works from Edda the Poetic Edda (also known as the Elder Edda) are not his. The poems were written by unidentified authors in order to commemorate the work of the older Norse poets, they provide extensive and detailed description of Viking mythology and culture.

The two poems in the collection that give the most comprehensive account are Voluspa (The The Insight of the Seeress) along with Grimnismal (The The Song of the Hooded one).

There are many different opinions regarding the precise dates for the poems. They appear to be in the same time period and are engaged in dialog and debate with Christian perspectives, and so the majority of historians believe that they are the product of a time in which Scandinavia as well as Iceland were slowly becoming Christianized. Their discovery altered and changed the way people considered pre-Christian beliefs.

The Prose Edda

The Prose Edda is the most well-known treatise on Norse poetry. It was published in the thirteenth century, following the time that Christianity was declared to be the main religion in Iceland and was written by Snorri Sainturluson. Snorri was able to base his Edda on poems from earlier times However, a closer examination finds that many the poems are personal opinions which reflect his worldview instead of a strict historical factual accuracy. Snorri also has supporters and critics among contemporary readers, however, on the whole it is illogical and unwise to deny his insight into the mythic stories from The Viking Age entirely, and the Prose Edda remains a valuable source of details. (Interestingly the name he used to describe the tales, Edda was never properly clarified.)

The Sagas

In addition to the extensive poetic sources The Sagas expand our understanding of the early Norsemen. Certain sagas, including the mythical sagas are based on mythology however, others describe the events of the period of migration, in which the initial Norsemen began dispersing across various regions of Europe and provide a detailed account of the early history of Icelandic families.

Despite all the plight of the Vikings only a little historical records have been uncovered from these tales and poems. The lack of information that is reliable has led to the varying individual judgments of historians over time to alter the truth of the Viking time period. One of the most unfavorable results of this is the long-standing image of Vikings as unreliable warriors who took and held captive innocent inhabitants of other nations. The raids that the Vikings did indeed, but it was not the entire story. Although it's not a lot however, the evidence of the past suggests that they were fascinated by exploring, and they had their own distinct tradition and well-developed mythology.

The Runestones

However, manuscripts written in writing aren't the sole source of information about the ancient civilizations. Archeologists continue the places historians have left off and the silver amulets of Thor's hammer, as well as different female figures discovered inside Viking graves have thrilled people studying comparative mythology all across the globe.

There is a reason why the Vikings created a variety of artifacts that will be of interest for historians and archeologists alike The runestones. These runestones show that the Norsemen during earlier in the Viking Age could, in fact, read and write using an alphabet that was not standardized, referred to as runor, which is from which we get the term rune. The alphabet was carved out on massive stones with raised edges, which were often coupled with intricate flowing drawings of wolves, warriors horses, and many other fantasic creatures. Runestones were usually vibrantly colored, but after many centuries of exposure to elements, there is no trace of these colors are left.

Also, the Norsemen are prolific authors. Approximately 3,300 runestones as well as over 6000 runic inscriptions have been discovered throughout Scandinavia alone. Runestones were also used to identify distant places from which the Norsemen were able to travel, and dozens of runestones are located in the Isle of Man in the west as well as across the Black Sea in the east and in Jamtland in the north along with Schleswig within the southern region.

Runestones were usually placed to commemorate the dead, however many have also been credited with great feats like the building of landmark buildings and monuments. Others commemorate economic and social achievements , and celebrate other important historical events. The most well-known runestones tell amazing stories of Vikings who were killed on journeys across the globe, but most are dedicated to the men who perished in the home.

A handful of runestones extend well beyond the deaths and lives of the famous Vikings. Their passionate, touching prose and captivating illustrations reveal an abundance of information about the history of Norse mythology and religious beliefs. For instance it is the Altuna Runestone in Uppland, an impressive effigy carved from blocks of solid granite, depicts Thor's daring journey to catch his quarry, the Midgard Serpent. With powerful prose and detailed illustrations the runestone recounts the story of how Thor was able to capture the serpent using fishing hooks that were baited with an ox's head of an Ox. When the serpent pounced on the ox's head the hook snagged inside its mouth, shaking it to such a degree that it rattled Thor's boat, and threw God of Thunder. Furious, Thor mustered all his power, held on to his fishing rod and then dragged his heels such a way that both of his feet slid across the bottom of the boat, and then down to seabed. It is remarkable that it is said that the Altuna Runestone even includes a representation of the foot that passed over the planks.

Another impressive piece of stone can be found in The Hunnestad Monument located in Scania It is a stunning stone with the image of the figure of a woman riding a wolf with reins that look like snakes. The stone is believed as a representation of the giganticess Hyrrokin (the one with the wrinkled, firey eyes) who was summoned to aid in the launch of the funeral ship carrying the god who died Baldr.

At the very least, one runestone is the Ledberg stone found in Ostergotland is believed to represent Ragnarok which is the mythical doomsday which is the time of the Norse gods. The Ledberg stone depicts a huge wearing, helmeted warrior believed to represent Odin The All-Father. He is surrounded by a beast of immense size that is believed to be Fenrir the monster Wolf-spawn of Loki Loki, the God of Lies that is believed to devour Odin at the end all of humanity.

It is interesting to note that there exists an entirely different kind of runestone that were crafted to serve a different purpose. A heroic boast, or, to put it in more simple words, boasting was seen as an acceptable behavior within Norse society. The characters of sagas are often seen engaging by telling the mead halls full of people of the creatures they had defeated and the threats they overcome, and the monuments they had constructed. A lot of Norsemen of the time have followed in their footsteps and literally thousands of them had monuments designed with the intention of immortalizing their achievements as well as their self-proclaimed positive qualities.

For example, a stone that was found at Rasbo, Sweden, is marked with a text that says it was erected by a man whose name was "Vigmund one of the most talented of all men" in honor of himself when he was alive. A second set of approximately 20 runestones were erected on the orders of Jarlabanke Ingefastsson the chieftain, who was to be quite content with making his marks on land which he owned, as well as causeways and bridges which he built "for his own reasons."

As Christianity was introduced to the Norsemen and changed the stories that they told on their runestones. In some areas, more than 50% of stone inscriptions have a connection to Christianity and in Uppland the region with the most runic inscriptions around the globe this percentage is around 70 70%. In many instances, explicit Christian symbols such as the prayer or cross were carved into runestones in later modifications.

When studying these runes as well as their Christian marks historians are able follow the expansion of Christianity across the Nordic areas. Some theories suggest that Uppland was the center of the region where the war between the old Norse paganism and Christianity first occurred. Since that the King of Sweden had recently converted to Christianity the chieftains as well as other tribal leaders from Uppland were likely to pledge their support for the King by showing their Christian faith to the world. they did this by putting Christian crosses and praying upon their runestones. Another theory is that it was just a popular fashion that gained popularity among the clans. Clans from Uppland were strong and well-established, as well as socially influential so the Christian designs they adopted were appeared on runestones that were raised by clans in smaller clans elsewhere.

As Christianity revolutionized the society and culture of the Norsemen and their society, so did it alter the stories written on the runestones. There were fewer and fewer runs that told stories of magnificent voyages and laudable deaths on distant battlefields, or told epic stories of Gods and serpents as well as the final days of humanity. Later runestones would make notes on the baptism of their subjects or laid to rest in their christening robes. They often explicitly invoked Jesus Christ as well as God as Father and the "light and the paradise" in Heaven.

Another way in which the runestones reveal how Christianity has changed Nordic society is evident in burials of the dead. From the beginning, Norsemen were often buried on runestones with notable figures buried near the runestones in their honor. Since the advent of Christianity The deceased were no longer burial sites near runestones in the wake of their ancestors, instead their final resting spots were located in cemeteries of nearby Christian churches. However, they remained prominent memorials in the homestead.

From the stories of notable (or simply wealthy) Vikings, to the epic tales of the mythological and gods as well as the advent of Christianity There is a lot the runestones provide us with information about the life that shaped people from the Viking people of Scandinavia. They are incredibly important in how we understand the prehistoric Nordic lifestyle and the changing beliefs, as well as a variety of tales of personal acts, characters and deaths are also revealed in the old runes.

Chapter 12: Viking Culture, History &

Warfare

For their victims along the shores from Britain in the British Isles and Northern Europe, it must seem as if the Vikings were a distant sight. They didn't, in fact and one of the lesser widely known facts about Scandinavian culture is that, as a group they Vikings lived for hundreds of years before earning the reputation of plunderers. Before that, the

Vikings were hunters, farmers and fishermen, as well as gatherers, fishermen as well as animal tenders - and a majority of them were.

Viking Life

Agriculture & Food

Despite their infamous reputation as thieves, the common Viking were farmers. Based on the discoveries of bones, seeds and other remains of earlier meals taken at Viking sites archeologists can provide a reasonable guess about the types of crops Vikings cultivated, the livestock they kept, as well as the foods and drinks they consumed.

The typical Viking male and female would spend the bulk of their time cultivating grain crops that could withstand the harsh long winters as well as the short, hot summers in Scandinavia like barley, rye and oatmeal. The harvests of the year were processed into flour, made into porridge, then fermented into ale. Viking farmers also cultivated a variety of cold-hardy plants like beans, onions and cabbages. To complement their diets they would forage taking natural berries, nuts and berries in the surrounding wilderness.

Certain Vikings also had livestock to raise including goats, chickens as well as sheep, pigs horses, and cattle. They provided eggs, milk, and the much-needed manure to keep the soil healthy. But the Vikings consumed only a small amount of raw milk. Instead, they made butter from it or made cheese with it and drank only the leftover buttermilk.

Naturally, and in particular when the harvest did not produce enough food to last through winter, Vikings sometimes killed their animals to make meat. The meat was simmered in a huge stewpot on an open flame or slowly roasted with an iron spit to become crispy and soft.

Fish and meat were typically preserved by smoking to be used later. It was additionally used in the preservation process of fish and meat as well as in the process of pickingling vegetable. The valuable commodity was generally obtained from trader on the move.

In the aftermath of particularly prosperous harvests, and at the most auspicious times during the season, Viking communities enjoyed lavish celebrations. The feasts were usually celebrated to mark seasonal holidays like those that occurred at midwinter and harvest time, and also during funerals. No matter the reason behind the feast, they were usually lavish that could last for an entire whole week!

They were usually accompanied by alcohol-based drinks that were typically consumed in drinking horns made of wood or made out of cow's horns. Ale, a strong beverage made from barley that was roasted, as well as high-alcohol-ice wine were both very popular.

The Viking drink of choice it was mead, an alcohol that is that was made by fermenting honey using water, sometimes using hops, grains or spices, as well as berries and spices. Mead was a very popular beverage, and so vital to Viking culture that it played an important role within their mythology. A good example could be the Mead of Poetry, which is, according to legend, made by the blood of the godlike being Kvasir. Consuming this Mead of Poetry was said to confer on its drinkers magical powers, increasing his intellect and turning him into a scholar or poet.

Towns and houses

Evidence of Viking settlements reveal that Norsemen constructed wall structures for their homes from whatever materials could be found locally, be it stone, wood or even the compacted turf blocks. Viking houses were generally rectangular, long and rectangular with roofs with slopes constructed of dried turf, thatch, or reeds. The simplest form of insulation is provided through wattle the lattice of woven wood coated with the thickest layer of mud that was used to protect against rain and wind. In the majority of Viking homes the floors were constructed a good distance from the floor and historians believe that this was done to keep the wind from entering.

It was typical to find Viking homes to consist of a single room that was used as a communal living spaces that were shared by all the members of the family. Families with more wealth, however, could have a smaller entry hall, a large main room, or even separate bedrooms, kitchens or storage rooms.

In the house, furniture were not plentiful. The typical Viking house was furnished with just a basic wooden table and benches on which people probably lay down and slept. The most significant feature of an Viking home, found even in the most humble of homes included the hearth, a secluded area where people could make a fire to provide warmth, lighting as well as cooking. Apart from the forge of the blacksmith in the village, the homes did not have chimneys. Instead, the homes featured a simple opening that let smoke out emanating from the fire. Without windows and no windows, the interiors of Viking houses were usually dark and dark lighting was often provided via the hearth, but mostly with candles or simple oil lamps.

After a delicious dinner of grain porridge, and strong barley ale the typical Viking did not have a private bathroom in which to flush his waste. The majority of the villagers probably used an open-air toilet or a censpit similar to one found archaeological digs in Jorvik. These were simply huge pits dug out of the ground, though they were usually screened with fencing to give at the very least some privacy. For washing, this was carried out in the wooden bucket or near the stream.

Viking settlements were bustling spots in which houses were constructed close to one another, creating an enclave of narrow, winding streets. But, due to the importance of farming grain that required huge open fields to plant crops, larger towns were not common in the Viking Age. There were only a few towns that were scattered across the rugged, cold Scandinavian countryside could possibly be classified as towns, and they were mostly located along the coast.

The harbor was the main area in Viking cities, since it was where merchant ships took off and loaded their loads of animals and goods. Markets were usually held on the quays, making it the main point of commerce. Quays were frequently the central point of town's business as as shipwrights, pottersand carpenters, leatherworkers, tanners as well as smiths and other tradesmen would often put up workshops close to the harbor, to cut down on the amount of time, effort and hence the expense to move their goods and their materials.

Clothing and Craftsmanship

Viking clothing was made from linen cloth, spun wool along with animal skins. The clothes they wore were heavily inspired by the fashions that were popular in England,

Scotland, and Wales such as long-sleeved tunics, trousers for men, as well as long dresses with women's apron. In the winter months it was normal for both genders to wear cloaks that were fastened with brooches. Viking women were covered with scarves or hats, as well as covered the head by wrapping their heads in fabric. It was also common for young girls to be bareheaded. Shoes, made of leather that was tanned or hardened were the most popular shoes.

The typical Viking outfit was designed to serve basic needs. Clothing was meant to keep one's body warm! However, Vikings did have some style and Viking clothes did not lack their decorative elements. Different natural dyes were utilized to dye fabrics: stunning blue hues came from the woad plant stunning reds from madder and yellow was derived from welding.

Despite what might be perceived as a flair for practicality but the Vikings weren't a strictly pragmatic group. Their skilled craftsmen made a myriad of beautiful intricate creations that remain even to this day. Typically, they were made of amber, jet, silver and glass, in addition to locally-sourced wood. Viking craft was admired for its beauty and intricateness of their design, as well as their long-lasting nature.

Viking crafts were particularly sought-after as goods for trade by non-Viking peoples. However, blacksmiths, carpenters, leatherworkers, and other craftsmen provided the market in the country with everything that a Viking required for their daily lives. Carpenters made planks for ships and shields for warriors and toys for youngsters; metalworkers made armor and swords for warriors, tools for farmer and the other artisans and jewellery for women.

We are aware about the quality and longevity of Viking craftsmanship from firsthand experience, as some of their works remain in use to this day hundreds of years following their creation! From the surviving pieces it is clear that the Vikings made exquisite jewelry in the form of necklaces, bracelets and pins, made of precious metals, particularly silver. Jewelery made from precious metals was typically used as a symbol of the wealth of the owner. The less wealthy people wore items composed of cheaper bronze or pewter, as well as silver alloys. Glass beads in necklaces were also popular with all genders. The most common designs on woodcarvings, jewelry and longships are depictions of creatures like wolves, and mythological characters like dragons.

From research of their settlements and homes they built, the Vikings weren't barbarians and relied on plundering their more civilized counterparts to get food and riches. Although the term 'Viking today conjures images of a wild warrior wearing in animal skins soaring into battle after a glorious battle but the truth was that the life of the typical Viking was quite similar to the agricultural societies that existed at the time. In other words, their lives were defined by a strict annual routine of sowing and tending their fields, cooking dry salting, smoking and pickingling food, and tanning leather or forging iron tools as well as dyeing or scouring the textiles that were used to make their clothes.

With the latest technological advancements such as the turbine and modern metallurgy in the distant future in the past, the Vikings depended in their hands, and simple tools to survive. Every day life was fighting against the harsh weather to provide adequate food supplies and provide shelter to all within the village.

Viking Raids

However, after a few hundred years of relatively tranquil existence that was followed by the Vikings started to gain their reputation for brutality. What happened that caused this radical transition from a predominantly agricultural society to one of a warrior's?

Many historians place blame on the pressures of the growing population in Scandinavia. Modern agricultural techniques and a short-term temperature rise helped the Vikings to produce more food and cultivate more of the land. The abundance of food contributed to healthier populations, longer life expectancy, and all in all, a steady growth.

The boom in population quickly collided with a lack of space. The terrain of Scandinavia is mostly isolated islands and rugged peninsulas, with limited space to expand. The majority in the landscape is insufficient for agriculture or is just too steep to be inhabited. This could have resulted in clan disputes among clans from across the border, but eventually it caused some Vikings to leave their homes to seek out and conquer new territories. In the north it was unhospitably cold for the majority of the year, and so enthused Vikings explored further towards the south, to east or even over into the Atlantic Ocean to the west in search of new shores to conquer and settle or simply to acquire things they could not get in their home.

Another popular explanation of Viking expanding was that the idea was a reaction to the use of force by Charlemagne and fear to Christianize pagan people. The ferocious battles he waged offered pagan tribes that were defeated the option of either baptism or execution. Vikings as well as other European pagan tribes naturally refused and sought revenge. In the end when Christianity finally gained presence in Scandinavia and the Baltic region, it triggered an intense conflict that split Norway for nearly 100 years.

Some historians believe that Viking raids were executed by exiles. The Vikings had clearly-defined laws were used to regulate themselves. One of the most common punishments for criminals who were convicted was exile. Naturally that was the case when criminals were taken away on a boat with a limited supply of food and told they couldn't be allowed to return they would likely have resorted the opportunity of plundering and pillaging nearby coastal towns to make ends meet.

In a way, Viking raids were simply acts of chance. England especially was experiencing serious internal conflicts in the midst of war. This meant that the majority of fiefdoms refused to provide assistance to neighbouring settlements with whom they were at war. Add to that the fact that a lot British towns and cities were constructed in the vicinity of the coast or river navigable, and it's evident that Viking fleets basically had freedom to raid or trade when opportunities arose.

A simple greed could therefore be among the motives behind Viking raids. The Vikings desired things that their neighbours had - coins and animals, slaves, spices treasures, works of art, and raw materials that they could not find at home. They may not have sought the same things as other cultures , but typically, they obtained these items through trade or diplomatic maneuvers. However, they were adept in sailing and were not afraid to combat, and at times they got what they wanted through pillaging and robbing.

One of the most famous Viking raids occurred in 793 when the Vikings attacked and plunder the Christian monastery of Lindisfarne located in Northumbria. For the majority of Britain the assault on an Christian holy place was a snare and, to put it mildly, a bit embarrassing. But unlike the rest of Britain it was there was a difference between the Vikings and the rest of Britain. Vikings were pagans and had no hesitation about robbing an Christian church. They believed that Lindisfarne was a simple and tempting targetsince monasteries at the time were typically filled with valuable treasures like jewels, books, gold, lots of drink and food, as well as cattle. Additionally, the monks living in these monasteries were not armed and were unable to protect themselves.

In the end, raiding was a element the Viking culture. Raiding may've begun as a simple grab-and-smash game however, over time certain Vikings were so proficient in their craft that they could become professionals, and began to use plundering and pillaging as their primary source of income. In time the practice of raiding and war grew into a way of life which grew in popularity and became a common practice until everyone male Scandinavian considered it an opportunity to gain personal wealth and boost his personal status by establishing himself in battle. The war became an integral aspect of their culture that each young Viking man was required to be tested during battle. It was thought that to die bravely in battle would be the sole way for one to rise into the hallowed banquet hall of gods. Valhalla.

In fact, the people of neighboring countries were afraid of the wrath Viking pirates who pounded the shipping lanes and coasts that sometimes stretched in a wide and far distance from their remote home.

Viking Weapons

According to the ancient legend that owned weapons was a right granted to everyone who was free Norse men, and was it was also an obligation of the social order. The importance of Viking's weapons in the warrior culture the fact that Odin the All-Father himself was quoted as saying, "Don't leave your weapons on the ground in the field. You don't know when you might require your spear in a moment."

Since battle and war were among the most highly regarded things an Viking could participate in and it is logical that the status of his social standing influenced the weapons he donned and carried to combat.

Wealthy Vikings dressed themselves in the spear, a massive round wooden shield or perhaps the sword. They were especially prized as status symbols and often handed through the generations through the generations from dad to son. The sagas also claimed that some swords were blessed with supernatural abilities. Similar to swords, only most wealthy Vikings were able to outfit themselves with the helmet. Other types of armor were very scarce and are thought to have had very little use except for Viking nobles, or especially highly skilled professional warriors.

Vikings with lower social standing like farmers generally armed themselves with the spear, shield, an ax, or seax which is a large knife. There was also the possibility of bringing hunting bows with them and used them to cut down an opponent's charge in the beginning stages of battle fights.

Armor

The wealthiest of nobles could only afford to wear armor, such as an iron helmet or chainmail tunics, though there were a few less fortunate Vikings were able to wear helmets made of hardened leather. Contrary to popular opinion, Viking helmets did not generally have ornamental horns, or wings that were adorned on the sides. (Historians attribute this popular and persistent myth to 19th century Romanticism.) In reality, helmets were made with robust guards for the eyes and on top of the nose for additional protection. Due to their limited supply the iron helmets were usually extravagantly decorated to show of wealth and wealth. Viking chainmail, used to safeguard the arms and torso, was constructed out of thousands of interlocking iron rings. It was highly effective at warding off attack with slashing, such as blows from the sword as well as blows produced by an Ax.

Shields

Shields were the most popular method of protecting against physical harm, and formed the initial (and in the case of many Vikings the sole) defense line within one's arsenal.

The most popular kind that was used in Viking shields was the circular shield. Viking myths indicate it was linden that was most popular material for making shields. However, evidence from Viking graves indicate that alder, fir, and poplar were the most frequently employed in the common usage. The particular woods were selected due to their lack of dense, making them light and easily maneuverable. They also were unlikely to break or split, unlike heavier, more dense timbers like oak. If the Viking shield would eventually yield to the impact of a blow the wood's fibers were prone to get caught between blades, preventing attackers from cutting deeper without applying significantly more force.

Additionally, Viking shields were often strengthened by putting leather (or sometimes iron) around the edge. Certain shields featured the solid center of metal, known as bosses, which offered an additional layer of protection for the hand of the bearer and reduced the risk of the shield being thrown away by the collision. Round shields differed in size, ranging from the 18-48 inches (45 to 120 centimeters) in diameter, however the majority had a diameter of between 30 and 36 inches (75 and 90 centimeters).

The most common tactic used in battle among those who fought the Vikings included the shield wall, also known as Skjaldborg. In this type of formation, warriors were positioned side by side with their shields. This way they formed a shield wall that was interlocked to deter attacks from enemies as well as missiles. When they advanced and aimed their spears at enemies the shield wall morphed into an intimidating attack formation that allowed the Vikings to pound relentlessly on the front lines of their enemies.

Another well-known tactic was the boar snout or svinfylking. In this tactic, warriors would form the shape of a wedge with the most fierce and most well-equipped of them making the top of the wedge. The boar's snout would take off headlong into the ranks of enemies with a slash, thrust, as well as cutting till they had exploded into the line of battle.

Archaeological evidence shows that Viking warriors loved their shields very much. They often decorated their shields with intricate designs and occasionally, elaborate silver and gold-plated metalwork was placed around the boss as anchors to secure the straps. It is interesting to note that there is an entire genre of skaldic poetry, known as shield poems. They provide descriptions of landscapes, patterns scenes, and patterns that are often drawn on shields. One of the most notable skaldic poem that dates back to the ninth century, called the Ragnarsdrapa describes how Vikings were known to decorate the shields of their armor with scenes from mythology depicting the wartime adventures and the deities of Valhalla. It is believed that the Gokstad ship, perhaps the most famous vessel for sea travel found in earlier in the Viking Age, has places in its hull railings that allow shields to be placed and secured. It is believed that when hung in this manner on the hull of a ship, the shields were used to protect the crew from the frigid waves and crashing winds from the ocean's high seas. There could have been a religious or superstitious value to decorating vessels with shields of the occupants who had been defeated.

Recently it was thought that Vikings also utilized a different kind of shield, the kite shield. It was a large, almond-shaped shield which was rounded on top and then curved downwards until it reached a point that tapered off towards the base. The name is a reference to the shield's distinctive shape that resembles the shape of a kite flying. For most historians of the present the shields of kites are linked to Norman battles, though it is believed that the Normans adopted the design of kite shields in the form of Vikings. However, to date there hasn't been any archeological evidence in support of this idea.

The Spear

Contrary to popular belief that the most popular weapon used by the Viking hoards was not the battle axe however, it was the spear. Spears were used most often by the Scandinavian peasantry, which comprised the ranks and line of Viking armies. Almost every document that survives of Viking raids mentions spears being used. They were able to be thrown in ranged weapons, as well as slashing , and throwing, spears were designed to Viking strategies and formations that required a high level of mobility and the capacity to adjust to rapidly changing battlefield conditions.

The standard Viking spear consisted of a spearhead of iron with a sharp blade attached to a hollow wooden shaft of 2 to 3 meters long. Spearheads could be in the range of eight to twenty-four inches (20 to 60 centimeters) and longer ones that appeared in the latter period in the Viking Age. They were usually secured to the shaft using pins. In some epics, characters are able to pulled out of the pin to remove the spearhead to deter the enemy from claiming it with their preferred weapon.

The sagas refer to a famous kind of hooked spear known as the krokspjot. It was employed for throwing. As a result, the spears that were barbed-thrown usually had lesser ornamentation than spears thrusting since they often been left unretrieved after leaving the hand of the thrower. Thrown spears also had smaller, more narrow spearheads to ensure it was possible to throw them further and with greater precision. The spears that had broad heads and heavier blades were referred to as hoggspjot or cutting spears. They were used to cut, slash and throwing in close-range battles.

Additionally, to their flexibility Perhaps the main reason for the popularity of spears is the fact that they can be constructed with lower quality steel, and more metal as opposed to other weapons like swords. This naturally resulted in spears being a far less expensive option, and also more easily accessible because even a common blacksmith from the local village could create spearheads in a matter of minutes.

Despite its appeal to the disadvantaged class, Vikings fostered a deep spiritual connection towards the spear. A magic spear dubbed Gungnir was the weapon of choice of Odin the King of all Norse gods, and also the God of War. The saga of Eyrbyggja recounts a tradition to throw a spear over the enemy's army prior to the beginning of battle. The spear was intended to guarantee victory by proclaiming it to Odin.

The Battle Axe

The ax came in a close second to the spear in the hand-held weapons used in the hands of Viking warriors. Also, the high price associated with making swords was the primary reason why the majority of Vikings equipped themselves with axes. Axes are however found in so many archeological sites that it is likely they were widely used, not only for weapons, but also as daily tools. This idea is supported by the finding of axes in burial sites of Viking women, as well as men.

A variety of large-sized axes made to be used in combat. Battle axes were equipped with larger heads as well as longer shafts for greater reach and potential for death. The most well-known, known as the Dane Ax, was as large as a man's and could be used with both hands. But the most feared was most likely most likely the Mammen Ax, which was ideal to throw and combat. When it was the Viking Age progressed and melee warfare evolved, battleaxes were able to be seen with more crescent-shaped edges that measured between 18 and 18 inches (45 centimeters). They were referred to as broad axes, also known as breioox.

The majority of known Viking axes had just one bit, and the contemporary picture of the berserker lying on top of his double-bitted axe is most likely a fantasy. But, Viking battle axes were extremely destructive weapons. Durable enough to be swung , or throw, the standard Viking Ax was powerful enough to deliver an impact to break the limbs, break shields and break heads.

Ax blades are typically constructed from wrought iron and had sharp edges made of steel they were also less costly to make than swords, Vikings were enticed by their preferred weapons. Ax heads were sometimes set with silver designs as were other parts of Scandinavian weapons, axes were often adorned with names. The Prose Edda reports that monstrous creatures like she-trolls were popular names for axes.

There is the Knifr along with the Seax

The Vikings utilized two different types of knives. Most commonly, the most popular knife, also known as a knifr was simple in design and was found in a lot of Viking burials. Even women, slaves, and even children have been discovered burials with the knifr that they had. Knifrs smaller in size were used for general-purpose tools, whereas the larger blades and longer lengths were probably used for hunting and combat.

Another kind that knife could be described as the broken back style seax. The seax was much heavier than the standard knife and was also used as the falchion or machete. A seax is a simple weapon, that had a single edge and a large blade. A wealthier Viking men may have bigger seaxes, some of which were big enough to effectively be used as an actual sword. Seaxes were less difficult to manufacture than swords, and the smaller seaxes would have been to be within the capabilities of any blacksmith who was competent enough.

The seax was widely used by the Saxons The seax was later inherited through the Vikings who established themselves throughout England and Ireland However, it appears seldom in Scandinavia.

The Viking Sword

An Viking sword was made to be operated with one hand and the other hand was used to hold the shield. They were double-edgedand had an overall length of up at 35 to (90 centimeters). In form and appearance it was a striking Viking sword was heavily influenced by the earlier Roman spatha. It was characterized by the grip was tight, there was no obvious cross-guard, as well as a lengthy, deep longer. Scabbards were made of wood, encased with leather and strapped to the right shoulder.

The cost of swords was extremely high to construct they were extremely expensive to make, and having an instrument was a mark of wealth and status. A single Viking story known as The Laxdaela saga, reveals that a specific sword had a value of half a crown which was the equivalent of buying a whole dairy cow herd.

The earliest Viking swords were made using an art of pattern welding. It required repeatedly twisting and joining sections of mild steel and iron to create a strong blade with a sharp edge. In later times, Viking swords were constructed entirely using a single kind of steel believed to originate out of the Rhineland. The grip of the sword was typically constructed from organic materials that included wood, horn , or antler and was then wrapped by a textile to provide better grip. Unfortunately this is why only a handful of Viking swords survived to be found by archaeologists of the present.

Due to the skill and money required to create the sword, Viking blades were often covered with maker's marks and inscriptions, such as "INGELRII" or "VLFBERHT" discovered on the blades of the time. Craftsmen frequently added their own unique artistic flair in the form of intricately decorated hilts. A lot of weapons were given names that highlighted their speed or their stunning appearance, like Leg-biter or Gold-hilt.

A sword was a sign that an individual Viking was a person with a high level of honor and respect for family members and friends. The sword was believed to possess magic abilities and lives of their own. Moreover, they were passed over by fathers to children. The more old the sword, the more valuable it became in value. Research of Viking burial sites reveals that swords belonging specifically wealthy warriors were occasionally "killed" before being placed in the grave together with their owners. To kill a sword, you had to bend and twisting it to the point that it was no longer usable. In addition to the symbolic significance of the ritual of dismantling an weapon by its user and killing a sword, it could also deter grave robbers from disrupting the burial place to get hold of one of these highly sought-after weapons.

Chapter 13: Viking Mythology

Norse mythology grew out of ancient Norse pagan religion and endured for many years following it was a part of the Christianization of Scandinavia.

Cosmology

Norse beliefs regarding the creation of the universe create an exciting and vibrant tale that held significance to Viking culture. Here's how the Vikings believed that the Nine Worlds were created:

Ginnungagap the abyss that is wide existed long before the creation of anything. This abyss of silence and darkness was situated between Niflheim which is the home of Ice and Muspelheim where was the place of fire.

The flames from Muspelheim as well as the frost of Niflheim began to move toward one another. With the sputtering and sound of the elements, the fire began in the process of melting the frozen ice. The resulting drops became an initial godlike gigantic Ymir. The hermaphrodite giant could reproduce sexually. If he sweated, less giants would emerge.

Audumbla A cow emerged from the frost that was melting. Ymir was fed by her milk, and salt-licks inside the ice helped nourish her. When she licked her lips her lips, she discovered Buri, the very first Aesir god. Buri later had an child, Bor, who went on to marry Bestla who was her daughter from Bolthorn who was a gigantic. Bestal as well as Bor's half-giant half-godchildren included Odin, Vili, and Ve.

Odin along with his siblings determined to take down Ymir. After they had killed him they began to create their own world using his body. The oceans were formed of his blood and muscles, his skin and muscle made soil. Hair made the vegetation, his brain created the clouds and his skull was the sky. Four dwarfs, which correspond to all four points on the compass kept the skull in the air above all.

Ask and Embla

Ask (also called Ask (also spelled) Ask (also spelled as Askr) Embla was the first human beings Their names refer to "ash tree" and "water pot according to Old Norse. After the Aesir gods were done making the universe they constructed Ask and Embla out of tree trunks that had been washed up on shores of the land gods had taken from the water. The gods were led by Odin gods, the gods granted the newly created humans the powers of the ond (breath which is also known as the spirit) and ordr (ecstasy which is also known as inspiration) and la. It is unclear what the word la is. Ask or Embla were also granted this world called Midgard which is our world to live in, as such, they became the father and mother of humans.

The tale of Ask the question and Embla is rich in significance. Naming the first man "ash tree and the first woman 'waterpot" links the first couple to both the water pot and tree. This demonstrates that masculinity and femininity are mutually compatible, reciprocal and intertwined concepts. This means that each is as crucial as the other to the ongoing flow of life. The same male and female duality is evident within Adam as well as Eve of monotheistic religions that are prevalent in the world today.

There are a variety of mythologies pre-Christian, with many apparently contradictory stories about human history. Some believe that people descend from gods. Some believe that human tribes originate from the groves of trees. The story of creation told by Ask and Embla Of course, the story integrates both these concepts The story informs us that humans are derived out of tree groves (washed in the shores in this instance) and that gods made them. This is a reflection of the Pre-Christian conception of gods and goddesses as invisibly forces that create things in the world of visible things as opposed to the concept of God of monotheistic religious beliefs. However, as Norse mythology claims that everything originated from the corpse of Ymir and Ymir, they considered that life itself stemmed from this single figure.

The Nine Worlds

The Nine Worlds are where the various creatures of Old Norse and Germanic mythology lived. Their realms were located in the branches and roots of the plant Yggdrasil. It is mentioned within The Poetic Edda, but there is no complete list of which worlds comprised the nine. In analyzing this as well as other sources that explain Norse mythology, one could create a possible number of Nine Worlds:

Midgard is the world of humans

Asgard is the realm made up of Aesir Gods and Goddesses

Vanaheim is the realm that is the home of Vanir divinities and gods

Jotunheim is the giants' paradise

Niflheim - the ice planet

Muspelheim The fire world

Alfheim The elf world

Svartalfheim The dwarf world

Hel - the realm of the dead, and the goddess Hel

Other than Midgard and Midgard, the other realms were mostly hidden from the eyes of humans. However, in line with the beliefs of the pantheistic and animistic faiths of the Norse and the Norse mythology, they were visible in various ways in the human realm. Jotunheim is an example. Jotunheim was a part of midgard's wild west. Midgard; Hel was the subterranean world beneath the earth; and Asgard was the sky.

The number 9 may also have an ethereal significance for the Norse. What exactly that meant has to be discovered However, the number is popped into several tales: Odin hung from Yggdrasil for nine days and nights in order to uncover the runes. Heimdallr was the son of nine mothers and before he was able to marry Gerd, Freyr had to be waiting for nine nights.

Yggdrasil

Yggdrasil (IG-druh-sill) is an Ash tree which is located in the middle of the universe. It grows from to the Well of Urd. Yggdrasil is the home of its own Nine Worlds within its branches and roots. The name of the tree may appear complicated, but it's "the ash tree of the horse Yggr'. The name Yggr is a reference to Odin and also has its own meaning The Terrible One. The name of the tree is more logical when you consider the tree was utilized to means of transport between worlds.

There's also that Well of Urd. Urd is pronounced exactly as it's written, means destiny. Therefore, you could refer to it as"the" Well of Destiny. In the well are three maidens, referred to as the Norns which we'll be discussing later.

In addition to those who reside within The Nine Worlds, other beings are found on, around the inside, under, and around the tree. They are briefly mentioned in the majority of books. The most famous are the eagle, which lives in the highest branches; Ratatoskr who is an animal called a squirrel, and Nidhoggr which is the most famous of the dragons and snakes. Ratatoskr is a messenger between bird and Nidhoggr. There are four deer Dainn, Dvalinn, Duneyrr and Durathror that eat the upper branches.

Midgard

Midgard is a reference to'middle enclosure' and is similar to the term 'civilization' used in modern English. It is the realm of humanity within all of the Nine Worlds, and the only one that is perceived, even though other worlds are interspersed with various parts of Midgard.

The word Midgard has a dual meaning for the term Midgard. It is located at the center of other planets, and is surrounded by Jotunheim wilderness. Similar to how these continents Earth have been surrounded by seas Midgard has also been surrounded by the oceans. And this is where Jormungandr resides. Aegir and Ran are also a part of the waters of Midgard waiting to claim the lives of seafarers in distress. It could be referred to as"the horizontal interpretation. The vertical meaning reveals that Midgard is situated in between Asgard as well as the Underworld. The axis is depicted by Yggdrasil which is which is where Asgard is situated on uppermost branch, Midgard on the bottom of the tree and underworld is located in the roots.

Both of these perceptions of Midgard can help illuminate the Norse people's mental picture of the world. They believed that the land that was considered innangard, which translates to inside of a fence is orderly, civilized and law-abiding. They viewed the land that was utangard which means beyond the wall that was wild and chaotic. These ideas had physical and psychological aspects that one's thoughts or actions could be innangard or utangard the same way as the physical geographical location.

In the Norse creation myth, when the gods used the body of Ymir to create the world, they utilized the eyebrows of Ymir to construct the fence around Midgard to safeguard individuals from giants. In a concrete interpretation of the legend, Viking farms had fences around them, to distinguish the inside from the outside.

Asgard

Asgard can be described as the place where The Aesir gods as well as goddesses and the literal meaning of Asgard is "enclosure to the Aesir'. The word 'gard' in the name refers to the Norse beliefs regarding innangard as well as Utangard. Asgard is, naturally an innangard. It is partially protected by a wall erected by Hrimthurs.

Asgard is situated in the highest point in Yggdrasil and is linked to Midgard via a bridge known as Bifrost. The most popular spots within Asgard is Valhalla which is the place where Odin is the ruler. Asgard has also been regarded as a shrine for the 12 gods, Gladsheim as well as their gods and goddesses. Vingolf. The gods gather in Idavoll each everyday in order to debate the destiny of all mankind and gods every day to discuss the fate of all men and.

Vanaheim

Vanaheim refers to the land of the Vanir'. The Vanir world is located within one of the branches Yggdrasil which is located below Asgard. The sources that survive are sporadic and do not provide the exact place of Vanaheim. The most reliable clue comes from it is stated in the Poetic Edda says that the Vanir god Njord travels east towards Asgard after being sent to Asgard as hostage. This would put Vanaheim in just to the east of Asgard.

Also, there is not much information about what type of location Vanaheim is. We can instead draw some conclusions from the name. In contrast to Midgard and Asgard Vanaheim, it doesn't end in 'gard'. like the other worlds, it finishes with the word 'heim'. Midgard Asgard and Asgard are both enclosed by fences, whereas the other worlds aren't and thus are utangards. This implies that the Vanir in Vanaheim have more naturalistic characteristics in comparison to Asgard's Aesir of Asgard and are more sophisticated in their culture.

Jotunheim

Jotunheim is pronounced YO-tun-hame. It means the 'world of giants'. This obviously, it is the place where the giants are in Norse mythology. Utgard is a different name for Jotunheim and suggests that this is a mixture between innangard and utangard. Jotunheim is an area of wilderness that lies around the modern world. the word "wilderness originates in the Old English root words of "wild-deor" which means "the home of self-willed animals'.

Within Jotunheim the giants reside on the peaks of mountain ranges within an eerie, thick, dark forest. It's always snowing and winter is never able to loosen its hold. The terrain is bleak and unhospitable. The river Ifing divides Asgard from Jotunheim. King Thrym was the ruler of the giants, while King Gudmundr resided in Glaesisvelli which is a place in Jotunheim. Jotunheim also ruled the kingdoms that included Gastropnir as well as Prymheim.

Niflheim

Niflheim or NIF-el-hame is the "world of fog' that is located within the Nine Worlds. It is the home of fog, ice, cold and dark. It is the complete opposite to the fire-filled world of Muspelheim. In the Norse Creation story, Ymir was formed by frost from Niflheim and fire was created from Muspelheim.

It isn't known much about Niflheim. It is only found in the works of Snorri Sturluson who utilized the word interchangeably with Niflehl that describes the realm of Hel. Niflhel is mentioned in earlier works, however it is very likely that Snorri created the word Niflheim.

Muspelheim

Muspelheim MOO-spell-hame one of the homes for the giants of fire. Muspelheim plays an important role in the making of the universe - as well as it is also involved in the destruction of. The moment the universe was first created the fire and ice joined together to create the first massive. The oldest interpretation of the word "Muspell may be 'the end of the world with fire'. It is a reference towards the Norse notion that, In Ragnarok, Surtr, a giant of fire, will emerge out of Muspelheim with a fiery sword to kill gods.

As with Niflheim, Muspelheim is found only in the writings of Snorri Sturluson. These works could not be authentically representing the pre-Christian Norse beliefs. The cosmological concepts, however they are able to be traced back to the earliest Germanic beliefs. The term 'Muspell' appears within Old Saxon and German texts and referring to the same ideas and ideas, meaning it has roots in Old Norse. Therefore although Muspelheim was the work by Snorri, it appears to have a pretty solid foundation.

Aflheim

Alfheim ALF-hame, which is "the home of the elves The place the place where the elves reside as part of Norse mythology. There isn't much information of Alfheim in the sources and it's only mentioned only in passing. The elves are described as gorgeous and bright people, which implies that their homes would be filled with light.

Freyr Freyr, one of the Vanir god was the Lord of Alfheim. It could be confusing to think to believe that a god would have the power to govern the elf world However, there's plenty of common ground among Freyr, the Vanir as well as the Elf of Norse mythology, and it's not too unexpected that Freyr is the Lord of Alfheim.

Svartalfheim/Nidavellir

The world of the dwarfs is known as Svartalfheim, Nidavellir or SVART-alf-hame. NID-ud vell-eer. It is a reference to the 'homeland of black elves' and 'dark field and dark fields', respectively. Nidavellir is likely to be the first name. However, Snorri was the first person to make use of the term Svartalfheim and Nidavellir is mentioned in an earlier source.

The dwarves were master craftsmen , who lived underground, and their world was probably the dark and baffling world of forges and mines and also the halls of incredible beauty and artifacts created by their craft. But, Snorri was unclear about the boundaries of Svartalfheim, and mistaken that the title of Svartalfheim's dwarf Eitri for the word "world" entire world. We only have a rough concept of how Vikings considered the homeland of the dwarfs.

Helheim

Helheim often called Hel or Hel, refers to the name used to describe the underworld. The goddess Hel supervises the earth. According to some sources, the dog guards its entryway, much like the dog guards in Greek mythology.

There is a connection between the Norse realm that was Hel along with the Christian idea of Hell are both named after the same god and were believed to be the burial place of the dead underground, however they had nothing other than. Norse beliefs regarding what happens following death aren't evident, however it is established that the place a person passed away was not determined by the way in which they had lived their lives.

The underworld is typically portrayed in positive or, at the very minimum, neutral terms. The underworld is described by some as a place where dead people would remain alive in some way or another, and it is often described as a place in which the life of the dead was plentiful even after the death. In Hel the dead spent their time sleeping, eating fighting, drinking and eating. It was not a time of eternal suffering or bliss, but rather the continuation of life.

The Snorri's Prose Edda is the only piece of writing that depicts Hel as a negative location. As we've seen, however, Snorri had a tendency to alter things by expanding the facts he could access. In this instance it is likely that he wanted to appear as the pre-Christian people of his ancestors pre-conceived the ideas of Christianity. There are few scholars who support Snorri's view of Hel.

Gods & Giants

Two gods from two races and one of giants, are the most important characters of Norse mythology.

The Aesir Gods and Goddesses

The Aesir are one of the two principal clans of the Norse pantheon. Aesir is pronounced ICE-ear and is the plural version of ass, which translates to god. These gods and goddesses of Aesir are a collection of figures that can be found in Scandinavian stories, such as Tyr, Baldr, Thor, Frigg, and Odin. They reside within the world of Asgard and are connected to the world of mortals in Midgard via a rainbow bridge called Bifrost. Asgard is one of the Nine Worlds and is located in the highest and sunniest trees of Yggdrasil.

The Aesir are part of a complex collection of mythological, cosmological and religious belief systems which are common to the Germanic as well as Scandinavian people. They first came into existence in the context of local culture forming around 1000 BC and lasted until Christianity arrived in the region between AD between 900 between 1200 and 900.

Although The Aesir had immortality, they proved much more vulnerable than the typical Indo-European immortals. The Aesir preserved their youthfulness by eating the golden apple of Ioun and could also be killed.

These gods and goddesses of Aesir as well as Vanir were seen as being contemporaneous, living alongside one and were not viewed as separate from each other. This contrasts with other polytheistic religions where specific gods were considered to be younger or more advanced. These two clans that were the Vanir and the Aesir were at war, exchanged hostages, and signed agreements with one another. It is thought that the distinctions between Vanir and Aesir represent the interplay which took place between various classes of Viking society.

Odin

Odin is among the principal, and the most complexcharacters from Norse mythology. Odin is the head of the Aesir clan, Odin is a figure who possesses both scholarly and warlike attributes, which are connected to the healing of death, nobility and knowledge, battle, justice and judgement, poetry, sorcery and other intellectual pursuits. It is crucial to remember it is true that Odin is revered by Norse and Germanic people through their entire history well in even the Viking Age. According to Old English, he was identified as Woden as well as in Old High German as Wuotan or Wotan. Many of the names for places in Scandinavia as well as Northern Europe refer to Odin. Even in contemporary English the Wednesday day of the week has his name. Although much of the information regarding early versions of Odin is lost over time, the most precise knowledge of him is derived directly from preserved Old Norse works.

In pop-culture representations of him in the present, Odin is often depicted as a battle commander and an respected ruler, but Odin was not like what was expected of the Norse. When compared to the great gods in war such as Thor or Tyr, Odin would incite peaceful people to a stale struggle with a sinister glee. While Odin was a god of war however, he was also a god of poetry and had qualities so powerful that they could have slapped shame on the warriors of the past.

He was known as an unpredictable trickster with zero respect for justice, fairness morality, morality, convention, or the law. And however, those who valued the highest honor, nobility and respect would frequently praise him. He was the head of the Aesir but the king was known to wander off from Asgard in solitary excursions or on self-interested pursuits. His patronage was saint of both kings and outcasts.

Odin was quite a bizarre mix of qualities. What is the best way to combine all the attributes?

Odin is a synonym for "Master of Ecstasy'. His name is broken into two components: 'odr' which means 'inspiration, fury, ecstasy' and the masculine word 'inn'. It is a specific article that means'master of'. Odin's ecstasy is the thing that brings together all the different domains he's connected to poetry, the dead, shamanismand wisdom, magic and warfare.

In the remaining Old Norse texts such as the Prose Edda, Odin is depicted as having a long beard with just one eye. He often is seen sporting an overcoat and a broad hat, while wielding his famous spear Gungnir. A variety of animals accompany Odin when he travels: the two wolves Geri and Freki and ravens Huginn and Muninn and Muninn, who serve as his scouts. They bring his news and updates from all over the world of Midgard. When fighting, Odin rides on an eight-legged steed that flies known as Sleipnir through the skies and into the underground.

Also called the All-Father Odin has numerous sons, but the most well-known is his god Baldr. Odin also played an important role in the creation of the universe by killing an ancient being Ymir and giving the blessing of immortality to initial two human beings Ask or Embla. In some of the texts, Odin is given a special connection to Yule as well as recognized for bringing poetry and runes to the world of mortals. Motivated by an unquenchable thirst to know more, Odin enjoys exploring the world in search of more and greater information, often hidden.

As a god of war, Odin did not concern himself with ordinary warriors He preferred to bestow his blessings on only the ones he believed merited his time. He also did not care about the motivations for the conflict or what the final outcome might be. He simply adored the chaos and raw energy of battle. This belief stems from his close association with warrior-shamans whose fights and spiritual practices were focused in forming an ecstatic connection with totem animals. Typically, these were the wolves and bears. And, by the extension, also with Odin himself.

Odin is in charge of the female-only Valkyries that fly over epic combats search of worthy souls who are worthy of being welcomed into Valhalla. Odin takes half of the people who are killed in battle. those who are accepted into Valhalla are known as the einherjar and are enticed to take in a meal and drink all they can as they prepare for the battle of Ragnarok the last great battle they will fight.

In later folklorestories, Odin is portrayed as the leader in the Wild Hunt, a procession of ghostly hunters that travel through the winter sky, which is thought to be an indication warning of war, death or disaster.

One of the main differences between polytheistic and monotheistic theologies is that in the first, God is viewed as all-knowing, all-powerful and loving. Gods who are polytheistic are not unlimited as are the people they guard. Odin saw the limitations of his abilities as something that he had to overcome. He did not hesitate to act in a cruel way to improve his knowledge, wisdom and power, but the way he treated himself as he was to any other.

Odin's Quests

One of Odin's main traits is his singular eye. According to legend, Odin sacrificed the other eye to attain the greatest knowledge. A few days later, Odin went into Mimir's Well. Mimir was a mysterious person, was a resident there, which was believed to be unique. Mimir had acquired this knowledge from drinking the water that was magical from the well. Odin asked Mimir to share some drops of water. Mimir was hesitant to share it unless Odin would trade his eye. Odin (either after a bit of deliberation or immediately, based on the particular version of the tale) wentuged one eye before dropping his eye into the pool. Mimir then put his horn into the well and then gave Odin the drink.

Another time, Odin set out to look up the runes. They are symbols carved onto the trunk Yggdrasil from the Norns. Odin was watching the Norns when they were carving these symbols onto the trees and admired their skill and strength. The runes are awe-inspiring to their Well of Urd, and they only display them to those who can prove their worth. In order to prove this, Odin hung himself from Yggdrasiland then stabbed him with the spear and gazed at the water that flowed from the bottom of the Well. He was there for 9 days and night, never permitting any other gods to assist the god in any manner, not even by offering water. At night nine, he started to see patterns in the well, namely the runes.

Odin was also famous for having obtained his Mead of Poetry, which will be discussed further in the book.

The death of Odin

Odin's demise is portrayed through the poetry Voluspa which tells of his conversations with a dead volva, also known as a shaman or wise woman. The volva shares with Odin (and consequently those who read it) wisdom from the in the past, for instance, the way Odin along with his siblings Vili and Ve provided life to the first human beings, Ask and Embla, and helped them live by giving them three gifts of the gods of three: Sense, Blood, and Spirit. Following the time that Odin gives her a cache of jewel-adorned necklaces and other jewelry, the volva proceeds to discuss Odin's role as leader and hero in the battle between the Vanir as well as the Aesir when they fought for supremacy over the realm of mortals of Midgard.

In the end, the volva predicts Odin's inevitable demise at Ragnarok. On the battlefield, Odin will fight against the enormous beast Fenrir who has grown so big that he'll nip Odin within his mouths, and swallow his entire body. A son from Odin's family Vidarr will seek revenge on his father by cutting the wolf's heart. After the world is consumed and washed into a flood then reborn as a lush , green paradise, the mortals and gods will gather to remember Odin's acts and recollect his runes from the past.

Thor

Thor was the most well-known god among the Vikings of Scandinavia. He was associated with thunder, lightning storms, oak trees as well as fertility and strength, Thor is a herculean personification of protecting mankind. He is the symbol of a reputable and faithful warrior, the kind of hero all humans aspired to be. Thor's physical strength is unparalleled and his conviction to duty and bravery is unshakeable.

With ferocious eyes with fiery hair and a fiery red beard, Thor is the son of god Odin and is the wife of the golden-haired goddess Sif. His most favored weapon is the Hammer Mjolnir as well as the other items of his magical collection comprise the belt Megingjord that will double his already formidable strength and his iron glove Jarngreipr and Gridarvolr, the life-giving staff. Thor is a warrior who rides into battle in an chariot that is pulled by two goats in black Tanngrisnir as well as Tanngnjostr that he kills and feeds to nourish himself, and revives.

Thor's most important task was to protect Asgard from giants who were usually the enemies of the Aesir. It's more than comical due to the fact the fact that Thor was three-quarters large himself: Odin, his father was half giant and Jord his mother was a full-sized giant. This kind of lineage was common among gods, and goes to demonstrate that their relationship with giants could be described as complex instead of a hostile one.

Thor also played an important role in the human fertility as well as farming. This is a logical extension of his role as a god of the sky who made it rain so that crops could flourish. The wife of his, Sif Shefa, also was known for her golden hair that is believed to represent fields filled with grain. Their wedding was one of the hierogamy which means the union of God.

Mjolnir

Thor's most famous item was his hammer with a short handle, Mjolnir, depicted in Norse mythology as one of the most terrifying weapons of the universe capable of levelling entire mountains with one hit. The word literally translates to "grinder" or "crusher" from Old Norse, and the Hammer is believed to be the embodiment of lightning in the same way that Thor himself is thunder.

Mjolnir was invented by the two dwarf brothers Brokkr and Eitri and the small handle was a result of an accident while making it. Legend has it that Loki offered the brothers his head that they would never create anything prettier than the products created from The Sons of Ivaldi. The story goes like this:

Eitri puts a pigskin in his forge and requests his brother to use the bellows until Eitri tells the forgeman to cease. As the fly, Loki bites Brokkr on his arm however the dwarf does not stop the bellows from working. Eitri then puts golden bristles that Freyr's boar has thrown to the forge and advises Brokkr to continue working. Loki is back and bites her on the neck twice. Brokkr manages to get through the discomfort. After creating Odin's ring Draupnir using bristles of gold, Eitri removes it from the forge, replacing it with iron, and then asks Brokkr to keep on working the bellows. Loki returns and bites Brokkr harder, and is able to bite the eyelid, this time making blood. As blood drips into the eyes, Brokkr has to stop using the bellows, so that they can wash it out. Eitri then takes Mjolnir out of the forge but discovers the handle smaller than it is supposed to be, causing the hammer cannot be used with one hand.

Despite this flaw Brokkr and Eitri remain winners of the bet. They are determined to take Loki's head however, Loki manages to negotiate to get out of the obligation by saying that they'd have to cut off his neck to retrieve his head however his neck was not part of the bet. To make things easier, Brokkr instead sews Loki's mouth shut.

Thor's Adventures

A large portion of Thor's adventures involves his riding into battles , and ruthlessly slaughtering his enemies or testing his strength by taking on a particularly dangerous adversary.

In the humorous poetry Thrymskvida, Mjolnir is stolen by the gigantic Thrymr who states that the hammer can only be returned if goddess Freyja is taken to him to be his wife. As a result, when the hammer is demanded, Freyja pointedly refuses and runs out of the room. In her rage drops her famed necklace Brisingamen. After some discussions Gods come up with an idea to send Thor to replace Freyja by dressing the man from head to toe in extravagant jewels, a veil-covered wedding headdress, dresses that fall until his knees and of course the necklace Brisingamen.

Following some initial protests, Thor is not happy with the plan and goes with Loki to Jotunheim The frozen kingdom of giants. Thor and Loki are met by Thrymr, who's created a feast of a lifetime. Thor consumes a lot of alcohol and food eating whole animals, and three casks full of mead. Thrymr is at opposite to what he expects of Freyja however Loki disguised as of a shrewd maid, offers the argument that Freyja's appetite is due to having gone on a fast for eight full days prior to the arrival of her husband due to her desire to meet her new husband.

When Thrymr raises the veil of 'Freyja's' in a bid to kiss her he's met by the terror of eyes that stare towards him with eyes that appear to be lit by the heat of. Another time, Loki perpetuates the ruse by saying that Freyja's eyes look like that because she hasn't had a restful night in her excitement. The giants then bring out Mjolnir to'sanctify the bride'and lay it on the lap of 'Freyja' so that the couple will be married. After seeing his beloved hammer Thor smiles with a loud grin, and then quickly grabs the weapon and slashes Thrymr dead, before brutally killing the remaining giants.

The majority of Thor stories end with bloodshed, however one notable variation is the one in Harbardsljod. Odin may be seeking to temper his son's arrogance pretends to be a ferryman, and arranges to meet Thor when he returns to the west. Thor when he meets the ferryman at the inlet, tries to gain access. The ferryman is unable to pass and becomes rude and inconsiderate to Thor. In the beginning, Thor manages to hold his cool however, the ferryman keeps blaming his victim, getting more hostile.

The poem turns into an exchange of words with a lively, humorous exchange among Thor as well as the ferryman. During the fight, it's discovered that Thor killed several giants and several islands of drunken women as he traveled in the east. After their argument, however Thor doesn't let his rage go and simply slaps the ferryman and strolls around the inlet.

Thor's enemy is the gigantic sea serpent Jormungandr which surrounds the human realm of Midgard. In one myth, Thor is to fish (for whales!) and baits his line using an ox's head of an Ox. Jormungandr uses the hook. With his incredible strength, Thor takes the serpent off the board and hits its head with a hammer. After a gruelling fight, the serpent is able to escape back into the ocean as Thor's friend cuts through the line. Thor comforts himself by carrying many Whales on his backs.

Thor's long-running feud with Jormungandr is set to end when they both die in the epic fight of Ragnarok. After that, Thor will again clash with the legendary Midgard Serpent, and although Thor will be able to kill that beast Thor is only able to take nine strides before succumbing its poison and sinking into the arms of the earth.

Loki

Loki the trickster god was not in charge of the specific aspect of life, but he played a significant - though not entirely clear - role in the world of gods. He's also often mentioned in many myths. He was simultaneously antagonist and an ally of Aesir and was simultaneously god and giant. He was the father of giant Farbauti while his mother was Laufey and Nal, could be a giantess, or a goddess, or other than.

Loki's complex and confusing times contradictory relationship with other Norse gods is different depending on the original source. In some instances, Loki appears to be helping gods in their quests however in other stories the gods are portrayed as being malicious towards the gods. His own personality is more consistent. Loki is an enigmatic, coward focused on the pursuit of pleasure and self-preservation. He can be helpful in general however, he is also a harbinger of an impulsive and sometimes even a bit snarky playful nature. He is also rude and very skeptical.

Loki's amazing guile and knack for sleight of hand are enhanced due to the fact he's skilled shapeshifter, having taken on the appearance of an hare, a salmon as well as a seal, a fly, and even an elderly woman in various instances. The ability to shapeshift lets him break not just the norms of society but as well natural laws. when he transformed into the form of a mare, he was his mother to Sleipnir Odin's eight-legged flying horse.

Loki also had kids in his personal body. Alongside the gigantic goddess Angrboda He fathered Hel, the goddess of the underworld; Jormungandr, the World Serpent as well as Fenrir, a massive beast - not a very reputable group. He also had his daughter, Narfi or Nari, together with his wife Sigyn.

Researchers have not been able to translate the name Loki. Many believe that the purpose will remain understood however, professor Eldar Heide has proposed an intriguing theory. He points out that some sources suggest that Loki to knots and that Loki was referred to as 'tangle' or "knot in Icelandic. Loki can also mean "tangle" or "knot"..

The Demise of Baldr

After having a tense relationship with gods for several years, Loki is ultimately condemned as a villain and thrown from Asgard. This is believed to be the initial step in the intricate sequence of events that leads to the demise of all Norse gods (and the entire world) in Ragnarok.

The story starts with Baldr who was the beloved child from Odin as well as Frigg. After waking up from a dream of his own suicide, Baldr was much depressed and confided the nightmare to his mom. Frigg was a popular figure for her in-depth wisdom about the past as well as the things to come she had also experienced similar dreams about her son's tragic death. In the name of love for her mother, Frigg used her vast power to command all objects across all realms to swear that she would never hurt Baldr. Every single one of them made the pledge with the exception of mistletoe, one of the plants Frigg considered too young to swear to an oath that was binding.

When he heard about that, Loki, ever the creator of mischief, created the most magical spear made of mistletoe. He then ran to the area where gods were basking in their new hobby: throwing various missiles at Baldr and watching the missiles fly off and not hurt the god. Loki gave his sword to god blind Hodr and he hurled it at Baldr. The magic of Loki guided him the spear killed Baldr who was killed in the spot where he was standing, in the midst of horror for the gods.

"The Tale of Loki's Binding

The gods finally revealed Loki's part in causing Baldr's death (and making sure that he remained dead, as we will see in the article in the article on Baldr). In addition, Loki had begun to criticize the gods in public. They concluded that his slander was too much and began to hunt him down.

Loki fled from Asgard and constructed his own home on top of the mountain. The house had four doors, so that he could keep an eye on his pursuers from all directions. At the time of day, he could change into a salmon and hide behind the nearby waterfall. At night

, he would sit close to the flame, making an net so that could catch fish to feed his family.

Odin however was able to recognize the place Loki was at the moment and the gods laid the scene for Loki. When Loki saw them coming towards his home, he toss the net into fire, transformed into a fish and disappeared in the water. When the gods noticed the fire-spreading net, they swiftly realized that he had a fish in his thoughts and concluded that he'd likely transformed himself to one. They made use of Loki's twine to make the net of their own. When they got to the river, they threw their net several times and each time, they just missed a big salmon. The salmon finally took an elated leap to the downstream, headed for the ocean. Thor took it from the air, holding it with his tail fins, as it tried to escape from his grasp (this is the reason that salmon have tails that are thin).

The gods drove Loki which was not a fish anymore, to a cave or rock; the accounts differ. The gods summoned two sons of his and transforming one of them into a wolf. The wolf killed and ate his other brother leaving only his intestines. The gods used these to tie Loki to the edge of the cliff or three rock

163

formations inside the cave. Skadi goddess of hunting put an animal just above Loki's head so that its teeth were constantly dripping venom on his face.

Since the time, Sigyn has been sitting with him, collecting the venom into the bowl. However, when the bowl is full, she must empty it and the venom then becomes allowed to spill out to burn the skin and he suffers excruciating pain. His shaking during these times is so strong that it triggers earthquakes that tear through Midgard.

The moment Ragnarok begins, Ragnarok, Loki will slip out of his binds and take his army of giants to an Apocalyptic battlefield. In the battleground, Loki will fight with Heimdallr, the God of War and in the ensuing battle they will kill each other.

Frigg

Frigg which means beloved is sometimes referred as Frigga. Frigg is the most prestigious Aesir goddess. The husband of Frigg is Odin and she is Baldr's mom. Despite her awe-inspiring stature however, there isn't much information about her deeds, attributes and character. In addition, much of what we know about her isn't unique since she shares many of her traits with goddess Freyja. Given the similarity between the two as well as the fact that they both derived from an earlier goddess called Fria It is not surprising that they're often misunderstood.

Frigg was a seer she was an Norse magician whose job consisted of determining what fate would be and then re-working the path. Also, she was a sorcerer. They would go between towns, and carry out rituals of seidr in exchange for lodging and food. As with most shamans, Frigg's status as a social shaman was not clear. She was simultaneously hated loved, revered, desired loved, hated, and celebrated by a variety of people.

Frigg had been accused of infidelity. It's reported that she was a slave who slept with her, and also had relationships in a relationship with Vili and Ve Odin's brothers who were put in charge when Odin was banished from Asgard.

Baldr

Baldr was the child of Frigg and Odin Baldr was the spouse of Nanna and father of Forseti. He was adored by all other gods and goddesses as well as his fellow Norse people. He was so happy and compassionate that he radiated the most radiant glow.

As was previously reported, Baldr met an untimely death as a result of the treachery and ill-will of Loki. The body of Baldr was cremated in a ceremony on the ship he was captain of, Hringhorni. His grieving wife, Nanna, threw herself in the fire to await for their final reunion at Ragnarok as was his horse, burned to death. Hringhorni was so full of treasures and gifts of parting from gods that gigantic Hyrrokin needed to be summoned to carry it out into the ocean. The wolf's birthplace was a massive wolf, Hyrrokin only barely managed the feat, putting forth enough force that sparks of fire erupted and the Earth shaking when the funeral barge released.

In a state of grief over Baldr, her son who was dear to her, Frigg sent Hermodr, the god's messenger to the underworld to plead with Hel to let Baldr go. The moment Hermodr came to the scene, he saw Baldr sitting right next the Hel in a position in honour. Hermodr was begging Hel to let go of Baldr and was so passionately did he plead that Hel was eventually convinced to some extent. Hel was given a condition to demonstrate she was sure that Baldr was truly loved all things in the world had to weep for him before she'd let him go.

And everything wept in adoration of Baldr The Beautiful... Except for Thokk, a giganticess that is believed to be Loki disguised. There are other versions that have Loki using a magic spell on Willow trees, who at the moment held its height and pride to stop it from crying for Baldr. When the willow was freed by the spell it fell to its knees in sorrow and has been weeping throughout the years. In any case, Baldr will stay in his tomb until Ragnarok. Baldr will then come back to life to cheer the gods' hearts in the final fight.

The Vanir Gods and Goddesses

The Vanir known as VAN-ear form the second family of Norse divinities. The name Vanir is likely derived from the word 'wen', which is the root of the word"which refers to pleasure or desire. The most well-known Vanir is Freyja, Freyr, and Njord.

The Vanir clan was a symbol of the wealth, fertility, as well as exploration. According to some theories it is believed that the Vanir were older than Aesir and could indicate that the conflict between the Vanir and the Aesir is an allegory of the societal and religious issues that are not fully remembered that were prevalent in early Norse culture. One scholar claims that the Vanir could have was a tribe of humans.

The Vanir reside in Vanaheim in the among Vanaheim, one of the Nine Worlds. They are more connected to Magic than Aesir. They participated in both endogamy and incest. This means they could marry without regard to their classes as well as within their family and outside of their family, which Norse society at the time strongly resisted.

Freyja

Freyja (meaning lady) was the most renowned and revered goddess from the Vanir tribe. She was associated with fertility, sex beauty and love, as well as wealth and war. She also died and became an honourary goddess to the Aesir following the conflict. Njord had been her father. her mother's name isn't known and most believe she is Nerthus. She has a brother named Freyr. Her husband was called

Odr. Many scholars believe that he's Odin Frigg's husband and some think it is possible that Frigg along with Freyja are actually the same person.

Freyja was a lover of things like beauty, material possessions and fertility, as well as love. Due to these passions she was seen as (to to use a modern phrase) somewhat of a party girl. The evidence for this can be seen in a poem, where Loki claims that she slept with all gods and elves around the world, including her brother.

As Frigg like Frigg, she was an expert in The seidr magic system. Her ability and expertise in manipulating desires, prosperity, health and others were unparalleled and she employed this ability to the benefit of both gods and humans.

Freyja could also be described as a goddess from the beyond, governing an heavenly field known as Folkvangr from her beautiful, large hall Sessrumnir. She selected half of the fallen warriors to reside there, the rest was to go to Odin's Hall, Valhalla.

One of Freyja's most sought-after possessions was Brisingamen which can be described as a necklace, as well as a torc (a type of a thick neck-ring) and described as being filigreed extravagantly bejeweled, and golden or amber in hue. Freyja rode in a chariot driven by two cats and loved her boar Hildisvini always close by. Freyja also wore an eagle feather cloak which could grant the wearer flight and even assisted gods by providing the cloak to them.

In the epics and poems Freyja's beautiful beauty is the reason that she is often the target of kidnappings. Usually, it's by powerful giants who want to have her as their wife. Freyja's husband Odr, the 'frenzied' and lost-in-the-moment god Odr often is absent from the home. Freyja grieves for their separation by crying tears of gold in his honor and occasionally embarks on her own journey in search of him.

A variety of plants indigenous to the Vikings who inhabited the land were named in honor of Freyja like Freyja's hair or Freyja's tears. After the victory of Christianity the name of Freyja was changed to the name of Mary, the Virgin. Mary.

Freyr

Freyr FREY-ur, which translates to Lord was a member of the Vanir. As was Freyja, his sister Freyja and his sister Freyja, he was an honorary Aesir when he was captured hostage during the conflict. He was among the gods most revered which is not surprising since it was believed that the Vikings considered that their existence and well-being depended on his existence and well-being. Freyr was the god of peace, prosperity, abundant harvests, and the fertility of humans. Naturally, he was the recipient of sacrifices at many times. The sacrifices during harvest festivals would usually feature a boar. It was his favorite animal.

Njord is his dad and his mother's name is unknown, but is believed to be Nerthus. Freyr loved a variety of goddesses and giantesses, among them one of them were his sisters, Freyja. (Incest was considered to be a normal thing within members of the Vanir clan, but not so among the older Norse as well as Germanic tribes.)

Freyr lived in Alfheim in the land of the Elves. There is a common belief that he was the ruler of the elves however there is no conclusive evidence for that from Old Norse literature. The real relationship between gods and the elves are sufficiently unclear to permit a variety of theories to be put forward.

One of Freyr's most famous belongings was his ship, Skidbladnir. The ship always had the most powerful wind and can be folded in such a way that it could fit in the size of a bag. Skidbladnir was an archetype of ships that the Vikings constructed for ceremonies that were not intended for seaworthy. On the land, Freyr traveled in a carriage pulled by boars.

Njord

Njord is pronounced NYORD. its meaning is a mystery. Like his two children, Freyja as well as Freyr, Njord is not just an Vanir but also an Honorary Member in the Aesir. Nerthus is most likely his sister and one of the mothers of his kids.

His name is often associated with sea-faring along with the sea, the fertility of the sea, and wealth. The Norse even used to have a phrase for people who were rich. They would have said "as wealthy as Njord."

Njord is the main character in the tale of Skadi. Skadi was a giantess who traveled into the Aesir to demand justice for the murder of her father. They informed her she could choose anyone god husband. She erroneously chose Njord and thought Baldr was his name. Baldr. They had a brief, painful marriage. A portion of their marriage was spent at her house in the mountains of snow that Njord was unable to take on. The remainder of their time was at Njord's house at the beach that Skadi was unable to take on. They soon separated.

Nerthus

Nerthus was a goddess worshipped by the gods called Mother Earth. The belief was that she participated in human activities, including riding in a chariot drawn by cows. Only priests were allowed to be near her or ride along with them in her chariot. They would be with her all through the day and have fun at any place she was able to visit.

If she went to a region there would not be war, no one would ever be able to take up arms the iron and its components would all be stowed away. It would be like this until the time she returned to her home. When she was ready return, all things - including the goddess herself would be cleansed by the lake. A slave would go through this ritual prior to being drowned.

Historians are able to link Nerthus with the Vanir by relying on her name. Nerthus is an Proto-Germanic name, could be known by Old Norse as Njord. It is believed that there are two explanations on why this happens. One theory is it is believed that Njord along with Nerthus are divinely paired and the second is it is because Nerthus together with Njord were actually one hermaphroditic god.

Gullveig

Gullveig or GULL-vayg is a goddess that appears in just two verses of the Voluspa. The verses recount the events leading up the Aesir Vanir War. in them , we learn the fact that she had been a seer. Gullveig was a traveler to Asgard and did magic which the Aesir believed was unsafe and unsocial. They attempted to take her down however, she was able to avert her death using magical methods.

Gullveig could have had more than just magic in her arsenal. Her name is comprised from two terms. The first, gull refers to gold, while the second, veig, is intoxication or alcohol drink. So, her name is something similar to the intoxication brought on by an expensive metal'.

Giants

The giants are an additional important category of beings from Norse mythology, having powers that are equal to the gods' two clans. Their character differs greatly from that of gods and generally, the giants and gods clash as antagonistic forces.

The English term "giant" is misleading as it conjures up an enormous-sized human. In the time of the pre-Christian Vikings the Vikings had more in common with dread beasts. The language of Old Norse they were known as jotnar and thursar which means 'destroyer' or "injurious one," respectively.

What made these devourers famous as giants? After William the conqueror ruled control of England at the time of 1066 French terms began to enter the English language. The most prominent of these was geant, which later evolved into massive. Geant was the term used to describe the demons of gods of Greek mythology. Later, over time, it was applied to Norse myths too.

Fenrir

Fenrir FEN-reer, who's name translates to 'the one who is a resident of the marsh' is the most terrifying of the wolves that is found in Norse mythology. Sometimes, he is referred to as Fenris the wolf, he's seen on several runestones and is present in literary sources. The father of his character is Loki as is his mom, giantess Angrboda. Jormungandr has been his cousin and Hel is his sister.

The gods erected Fenrir within their stronghold however, they were so terrified of Fenrir they decided that Tyr could be the one who was brave enough to feed Fenrir. As Fenrir increased in strength and their fear grew, so did theirs and eventually they made the decision to tie Fenrir. They made him fall into a chain of chains, declaring to him they wanted to gauge the strength of his character, and would yell each break and they would tremble inwardly.

Then they visited the Dwarves and asked them to make an iron chain that could not be broken. They made the chain out of bird spit and mountain roots, fish breath and a beard of women, and footsteps of the cat. The chain was referred to as Gleipnir which means 'open'.

Fenrir had doubts when presented with Gleipnir So he demanded that gods or goddesses place their hands on his mouth to signify of trust. Tyr offered to help and, when Fenrir discovered that he could not escape, he licked Tyr's hand. The gods then dragged Fenrir to a deserted region and bound him to a stone with a sword, putting it in the mouth of his to prevent it from closing. While he yelled and sat in a trance, a river called Expectation came out of his mouth. He'll stay at the mouth until Ragnarok.

Skadi

Skadi SKAHD-ee a giantess born and a goddess through marriage. Her name could be a reference to the word skadi which means harm, or could be derived from skadus, which means shadow. Most likely , it's related to Scandinavia however it is uncertain if she has lent their name to that area or in the reverse.

Her home is on the highest point of the mountain in which you can always find snow.

She is well-known for her hunting skills and is rarely not mentioned without her snowshoes, skis and bow.

The giants are mostly the source of darkness and death, Skadi did receive the status of Goddess when she was married to Njord as well as being the object of worship during the Viking Age. This suggests that she might be more generous than her family.

Jormungandr

Jormungandr, YOUR-mun'-gand, is known as a sea snake and his name is a reference to "great beast". He is so large that his body is encircling Midgard completely and has earned him the names for Midgard Serpent or World Serpent. He is the son of Angrboda and Loki and his two twins are Fenrir and Hel.

Thor is his arch-enemy. they've fought several occasions, and eventually end up killing each other in Ragnarok. Jormungandr is a recurring aspect of Germanic religious traditions, and Germans traditionally blame the god for earthquakes.

Nidhoggr

Nidhoggr is yet another famous serpent. His name translates to 'curse-striker'. He dwells below Yggdrasil and eats the roots of the tree, and this harms the tree and aids in Nidhoggr's purpose of dragging the earth into chaos. This suggests that he played an important part in the creation of Ragnarok and in the course of the battle, the king will take flight across Yggdrasil to fight with the giants. There are parallels drawn between Nidhoggr as well as the biblical serpent from Eden. Garden of Eden.

The Great War

The majority of Norse mythologies, it can be difficult to discern what gods, goddesses, and gods are related the Vanir and which belong to the Aesir. There is one instance when it is simple to discern the distinction: the war between the Vanir and the Aesir.

Freyja Freyja, an ancient Vanir goddess, travelled to Asgard with as her title Heidr. She dazzled her fellow Aesir gods as well as goddesses by their power and initially they were eager to avail her services. After a time they realized that they had abandoned their beliefs of loyalty to kin and respect for their own desires. They blamed Freyja for their troubles They tried three times to execute her by burning the body, but every time she was born again.

The incident sparked hatred and fear among the two god clans and swiftly resulted in a war erupting. The Aesir engaged in battle using weapons and force, whereas the Vanir employed magic. The war lasted several years as each side gained an advantage at different places.

Then, both sides got exhausted from fighting and declared an end to the war. In accordance with the customs of the day the clans paid respect to its rival by releasing hostages to live together. For instance, the Vanir delivered Njord, Freyr, and Freyja to Asgard as hostages, while Asgard's Aesir also sent Mimir as well as Hoenir for Vanaheim.

Njord and his family were blessed with an essentially peaceful life in Asgard. It's not the same about Mimir as well as Hoenir. Hoenir and Mimir Vanir soon realized Hoenir could provide them with fantastic guidance on any subject however, they did not realize that it was only true in the presence of Mimir along with him. Actually, Hoenir was a slowwitted person who was a sloppy bloke who had no idea what to say, unless asked by Mimir. After Hoenir had stated to Mimir to Vanir "let other people decide" several times and they started to believe that they were cheated during Hostage exchange. They cut off Mimi's head and returned it to Asgard. Through chanting and embalming it in herbicides, Odin could keep Mimi's head to ensure that he was capable of receiving assistance in situations in need.

But there was no way that the gods were interested in reviving the conflict over this particular incident. Instead they all joined together and spat out in the cauldron to pledge to maintain harmony among them. Their saliva produced Kvasir who was the most wise of all creatures.

Ragnarok

Ragnarok refers to the 'doom of gods'. It is the name the Norse gave to the final ending of their cosmic system and the later resurrection.

The prophecies and dreams of the past had forecasted the demise of the universe and all living within it. When the first prophesied prerequisite for the demise of Baldr occurred Gods had to confront the reality that they could not be able to escape their fate. Odin began to bring the most skilled human warriors in Valhalla to aid him in the final fight to defeat the beasts. However much they plan for battle, the gods knew they could not avert their end.

As Ragnarok is nearing and the people of the world begin to be forced to change their lifestyle and sink into a state of deep depression. This is the same to the gods. A lot of people break oaths, and fail in other ways. Then , three winters will follow and one right after the next without a summer in between them. The brutal dark and frigid winter is called Fimbulwinter. It is also known as the Great Winter.

Conclusion

Despite their bloody history the Vikings have found their appearance in the minds and imaginations of craftsmen in the present day. Their brutality and rage has been the subject of many epic stories and popular stories that have endured the test of time.

Contrary to popular belief that they were a cult, the most important thing to keep in mind about them is that they were trying to keep their lives in a dangerous period. Religions were just beginning to take hold of our minds and in the hearts of the people. Only the most powerful were certain to endure; and they did.

They weren't as savages, as the some media portray them. The were civilized group with their own rules and laws to protect their culture.

They were also not just warriors. They were also poets, farmers scholars, scholars, shamans politicians, and students. Rallying and pillaging was just one aspect of their lives. They were a fun-loving group, but they also faced some challenges.

In closing avoid any belief that Vikings were unclean warriors who were wearing helmets with horns. A lot of historical evidence points the normal design of helmets without horns. Their helmets were constructed of metal and were covered with animal skins, or other metals to protect their heads.

Additionally the excavated Viking objects show that they were proud of their appearances. They used combs and brushes with which they could fix their beards and hair.